CHAPTER ONE

The arrival of three new medical men at St. Bede's Hospital sent a tidal wave of excitement surging through the wards. Even the patients felt a subtle change in the atmosphere, a quickening of the hospital pulse underlying the mechanical efficiency of the nurses.

For changes in the medical staff of this old-established hospital were rare; so rare that few of the nurses could remember the advent of even one new doctor, let alone three. A new visiting surgeon, a new pathologist, and a new house physician made a triple dose of excitement.

'Just imagine!' breathed Nurse Warren in the kitchen of Luke's Ward. 'Three *gorgeous* new men!'

Nurse Warren ('Bunny' to her contemporaries) was an incurable romantic. Not so Sister Parker ('Nosy' to her subordinates), who sniffed and said caustically: '*No* men are gorgeous, Nurse. They are unfortunate evils which a malignant fate forces women to endure. Now get on with those diet sheets and let me hear no more gossiping this morning!'

And she swept out of the ward kitchen, her stiff apron rustling like dry leaves in the wind. Nurse Warren threw a pitying glance at her retreating figure and whispered hoarsely after she had gone: 'I swear the starch from her uniform has spread into her heart, if she has a heart, which I doubt.'

'She must have,' ventured a student nurse anxious to air her knowledge, 'otherwise the blood stream could not circulate from the auricle to the ventricle.'

Bunny Warren groaned: 'You must be Sister Tutor's pride and joy, my child! Believe me, if old Nosy has a heart it can be nothing more than a mechanical pump to keep the breath of life in her body. What for, I don't know.'

Staff Nurse Connell checked a smile and, forcing a note of authority into her warm, friendly voice, said: 'That's enough, Bunny. Nurses should never be disrespectful toward their superiors.' She averted her face as she said that. 'And you heard what Sister said about gossiping. I echo it.'

But she echoed it half-heartedly, Nurse Warren knew. Like everyone, she thought the world of Staff Nurse Connell and would do anything for her. She liked her sincerity and lack of affectation, her kindness and humor and optimism. In short, she liked everything about her—including her looks, which any girl would be justified in envying. Hope Connell was as vivid as a flame, her titian-red hair seeming to draw its life from her bright spirit. It was warm, copper-colored hair, reflecting the sunniness of her nature.

SISTERS IN NURSING

SISTERS IN NURSING

Rona Randall

This Large Print book is published by BBC Audiobooks Ltd, Bath, England and by Thorndike Press®, Waterville, Maine, USA.

Published in 2005 in the U.K. by arrangement with the author.
Published in 2005 in the U.S. by arrangement with Juliet Burton Literary Agency.

U.K. Hardcover ISBN 1–4056–3156–2 (Chivers Large Print)
U.K. Softcover ISBN 1–4056–3157–0 (Camden Large Print)
U.S. Softcover ISBN 0–7862–7022–5 (Nightingale)

The text of this Large Print edition is unabridged.
Other aspects of the book may vary from the original edition.

Set in 16 pt. New Times Roman.

Printed in Great Britain on acid-free paper.

British Library Cataloguing in Publication Data available

Library of Congress Control Number: 2004111184

'You must have been christened Hope because you're so darned cheerful!' Bunny Warren had once commented. 'The complete optimist, that's you! And bless you for it! What St. Bede's would do with without you, Luke's ward in particular, I can't imagine. Every nurse would walk out.'

Hope laughed at that, as she laughed at most things. Nevertheless, she was an intelligent girl and one who could be serious enough when occasion demanded. Otherwise she would never have reached the position of staff nurse in a hospital like this.

St. Bede's was not a large establishment, but a small, intimate place conducted on more personal lines than the larger state institutions. As a result, the nurses had more to do—more domestic chores and drudgery—than would have been their lot in a big hospital, where ward orderlies were employed specifically for the menial tasks. Nevertheless, few nurses left St. Bede's. Whether this was due to the splendid training they received there, or to the feeling of 'belonging,' of being part of one big family rather than a mere cog in an immense wheel, no one knew. If anyone had asked a St. Bede's nurse why she did not turn longing eyes toward the metropolitan hospitals, with their splendid nursing conditions and active social life, she would have been unable to answer. The same applied to the medical staff. Vacancies for doctors occurred only upon death or retirement, which was precisely the situation now.

Old Doctor Walker, the hospital's chief pathologist for over twenty years, had finally retired through ill health. Dear old Mr. Entwhistle, the easygoing, kind-hearted, white-haired surgeon, had, to everyone's grief, died suddenly. The senior physician had finally retired for the simple reason that he was too old to give of his best, and realized it. This meant promotion for the man under him and a consequent vacancy at the lower rung.

Thus three unknown medical men were due to descend upon the hospital forthwith. Such a situation was unprecedented and excused, in Staff Nurse Connell's eyes, the nurses' thinly veiled excitement. She regarded Bunny Warren's frank young face with friendly understanding. Bunny was no beauty, but a lovable girl.

Hope said indulgently: 'Would you like to run up to the path. lab. for the Harvey test meal?' and was rewarded by a beaming, grateful smile.

'*Would* I! Connell, you're an angel!'

'Not yet, I hope. But hurry, won't you? Sister will be back at any moment, and she will expect it to be here.'

In one bound, Bunny was through the door. Outside in the passage she steadied herself. A nurse should never run when on duty—it was forbidden by all the laws of nursing.

Nevertheless, her feet itched to break into a trot, for this was an opportunity every other nurse would envy—the chance to get up to the pathological laboratory and have a good look at the new man.

Hope's head appeared through the swinging door of the kitchen and called after her softly: 'And tell that sister of mine that it should have been sent down half an hour ago, Nurse!'

'Golly, I wouldn't dare talk like that to any member of the lab. staff!'

Hope chuckled: 'Why not try it on the new pathologist and report on his reaction?'

She withdrew, and Bunny hurried on to the main hall. By the staff elevator a girl was waiting. She wore a white coverall and she stood very still, with a quality of repose rare in one so young. Her eyes were clear and steady and very beautiful—as, indeed, was her face. She wore her hair in a smooth, simple style, swept into a coil in the nape of her neck. It was the color of ripe corn.

Nurse Warren said: 'Hello, Charity—going up?'

'Yes, I've pressed the button. The elevator is coming now.'

The little wooden cage slid to a standstill and Bunny opened the doors. 'In you go!' she cried gaily. 'What floor, ma'am? Lingerie, hosiery, corsets?'

The girl in the white coverall laughed. It was a warm laugh, radiating happiness. Bunny said:

'I suppose you want the third? Whom are you walloping today, Miss Connell?'

'A patient from one of the private wards. Caroline Ransom.'

'Wow! We *are* stepping high these days! Society, eh? Wasn't she one of this year's debs?'

'I believe so.'

'What is she doing in St. Bede's?'

'Injured her leg when hunting—nothing serious, but it is being a bit stubborn. So is she. She bitterly resents having to come along to my room for treatment; insisted that I should go to her. I tried it the other day, but her bed table was so cluttered with things, which she positively refused to have removed, that I was petrified all the time lest I send anything flying. Finally I did. A vase of expensive roses. She blamed the nurse for leaving them there, as well as me for knocking them over. A junior nurse, too, which I thought unkind. The child said later that Miss Ransom wouldn't allow her to move them before the treatment commenced. I believe her.' The girl sighed philosophically. 'I suppose such patients are sent to try us! And at least the result has been satisfactory, from my point of view—she won't have me at her bedside any more, which means she has to come to me this afternoon.'

Bunny said indignantly: 'And a good thing, too! From all I hear, she seems thoroughly spoiled. I imagine she trades upon the fact that

Lady Ransom was on the Board of Governors before the National Health Scheme came along. I gather the Ransoms still regard the place as their hospital! Well, I'm glad I'm not up in Mark's ward. I hear she has all the nurses running—as if they haven't enough to do in the main ward without attending to her non-stop private bell! If she were really ill she wouldn't have the strength to ring it. Here we are—third floor, ma'am!'

'Where are you going, Bunny? Shouldn't you be in Luke's?'

'Thanks to your sweet sister, I'm off on a wild adventure—going to give the new pathologist the once-over.'

Charity Connell stepped out of the elevator. 'If you see Faith, tell her I may be late for supper. Ask her to tell Home Sister, will you?'

'Of course. What's keeping you?'

'Matron wants me to massage her leg, and it can only be done when she comes off duty.'

'Poor old battle-axe! What's wrong?'

'Rheumatism. And standing doesn't improve it. And she isn't a battle-axe, you know. She has a heart of gold, as Faith and Hope and I know.'

She waved her hand—a sensitive hand—turned neatly, and departed. Bunny shut the lift gates and pressed the top floor button. Charity Connell walked down the long corridor to the physiotherapy quarters, unaware of a man coming toward her. He was tall and dark, with a strong face and a bitter mouth. Too bitter a mouth, thought matron, who walked beside him, in one so young.

Seeing Charity she said: 'Ah, Miss Connell—let me present our new home physician, Doctor Shearing. You will find Miss Connell a loyal ally, Doctor, and positively tireless. I've known her to treat as many as ten patients in a day, and the treatment of the last has been as thorough as the first.'

'Indeed?' said Michael Shearing politely. He was glad to hear the hospital had an efficient physiotherapist, but quite indifferent about her as a woman. He had no time for women. His early memories were bitter ones as far as the opposite sex was concerned, thanks to the disillusionment his mother had caused him at a most impressionable age. After that, his upbringing had been entirely masculine, free of all feminine influence, and for that he was thankful. After the divorce, his father had withdrawn from women—silent, embittered, unforgiving—and his schoolboy son had grown up, inheriting his hatred and nursing forever the memory of a mother he had adored forsaking him.

But that was a story locked away in the secret recesses of his mind.

The tall blonde girl regarded him with her clear, disconcerting gaze.

He held out his hand, but to his surprise she ignored it. There was an awkward little moment as he stood there, hand outstretched, aware that here was at least one woman who did not regard him with arch speculation. Well—that suited him. He dropped his hand, and Matron said something to the girl swiftly, as if to cover the moment, about coming along to see her at six-thirty. He waited with suppressed impatience while they talked, which was actually only for a minute or two, but, in the opinion of a man who was eager to be about his business, even that was too long. Then the girl inclined her smooth blonde head in farewell and went on her way. As she passed him a remote, detached part of his mind registered the fact that her walk was singularly graceful.

CHAPTER TWO

Entering the pathological laboratory, Bunny Warren saw the dark head of the third Connell sister, stooping above a condensing flask. They were actually triplets, Faith, Hope, and Charity Connell, but Faith had preceded Hope into the world by precisely half an hour, and perhaps it was even this brief seniority which had made her the maternal one of the trio.

Whatever the reason, Faith was the serious one—intense and dark, beautiful when she smiled. The trouble was that she smiled so rarely. Her sweet, serious face regarded the world with an air of wistful solitude. She felt intensely responsible for her two sisters—perhaps this was due to the tragedy which succeeded their birth. Matron had tried to coax her into gaiety as a child, but rarely succeeded. Matron, had indeed made herself responsible for the upbringing of the three Connell girls—a responsibility which St. Bede's itself understood and shared, for Doctor Connell, their father, had been a promising member of the medical staff.

Matron, then staff nurse in John's ward, had been young Mrs. Connell's greatest friend, promised godmother of her children. She had helped the young couple at the time of the babies' arrival, lending a hand with the triple amount of nursing whenever she was off duty—and loving it. The Connells had occupied married quarters in the hospital, David Connell being a junior member of the staff. The future, of which a motor accident had deprived him, had been a promising one, but at the time of his death he had been firmly established only on the lowest rung. Therefore, the only legacies David and Stella Connell had been able to leave to their children were the characteristics symbolized by their names—faith, hope, and love. Better legacies by far, thought Matron, than all the material possessions in the world.

It was she herself who had christened them

thus; Stella's choice had remained unknown. The children were precisely three weeks old when their parents were killed. Matron herself had been 'sitting' with them while David took Stella for her first outing—a run in his shabby little second-hand car one Sunday evening. An oncoming car, racing recklessly along a wet high road skidded and smashed the little second-hand car into splinters.

Even now, Matron could remember the horror of that moment—the moment when the news came to her. She'd been sitting with her feet up, knitting; her hair, which was then dark, loosened about her shoulders. She was listening to the Evensong broadcast; the babies were sound asleep in an adjoining bedroom. It was John Benham, then a shy clerk in the secretary's office, who had brought her the news. John had called to walk back with her to the nurses' home. He'd told her beforehand that he 'had something important to ask her,' but as he entered the hospital the news of the accident was just coming in, so whatever he had been going to ask her simply had to wait. She didn't go back to the nurses' home that night. She stayed with the three Connell children.

It was one of those moments which seem too terrible to be real; only the voice of the preacher, coming from some distant church, called her back to reality. His words echoed in the silent room.

'And now abideth Faith, Hope, and Charity . . . these three . . .'

And, forever after, that was how she thought of Stella's children. It seemed the most natural thing in the world to have them christened thus, when the time came.

Not one second of that hour was ever obliterated from Matron's mind. Not even John Benham's face as he looked at her, listening to what she had to say. 'They are mine, John—they will always be mine. I shall dedicate my whole life to looking after them.'

'There will be no room in it for anything else?' he asked quietly.

'Nothing else but my work. I *must* work—for them.'

'They are not your responsibility! Relations must look after them!'

'They have no relations. Both David and Stella were only children—only children *of* only children. The babies are absolutely alone in the world, except for me.'

He said nothing more. She could see in his eyes that he understood, and agreed. But he never asked her the important thing—the thing he had come that night to ask. Instead, he had remained in the background of her life—a bulwark of strength, an unfailing friend. They had neither of them married.

*　　*　　*

Nurse Warren said in businesslike voice: 'Nurse Connell sent me up for the Harvey test meal. Sister wants it.'

Faith Connell's head lifted. Her hair was a dark and lovely cloud, her eyes deep-set and intensely blue. Although their features were very much alike, each sister's coloring was different, making them easily distinguishable. There were, of course, other things which marked their separate personalities; Faith's seriousness, Hope's gaiety, Charity's gentleness. But each was lovely to look at in her own particular way.

The distillation which Faith had been studying went on bubbling in the condensing flask, writhing like a colored snake through a maze of transparent tubing. She switched it off, looked across the room at Bunny, and said: 'It's ready—over there in the container. I was going to send it down. Then I started on this job, hoping to get it done by the time the new Chief arrived . . .'

'Oh—hasn't he come?' Nurse Warren's tone was disappointed.

'Not yet. Of course, he'd report to the superintendent's office first. That would delay him. I must say it suits me—I haven't got this room ready properly. Old Doctor Walker liked his table over there, against the wall, but the new man has sent all sorts of instructions as to how he wants things arranged. He sounds terrifying—and fussy!'

'Whatever is this?' Bunny regarded an enormous deal table, crowded into one corner, with horror. Faith smiled briefly. 'That,' she said, 'is the new pathologist's work table, believe it or not.'

'It looks as if he means business!'

'Or to spread himself out . . . I rang the theatre first thing this morning to see if I could borrow an orderly, but, needless to say, he hasn't turned up. The lab. boy and I have tried moving this table between us, and can't. Why is the operating theatre the only department in this hospital which is allowed male orderlies?'

The door opened abruptly and there, to Faith's relief, stood the theatre orderly.

'Thank goodness you've come!' she cried. 'I must say you've been long enough about it!' She regarded his immaculate coverall wryly. 'That is going to be messed up in no time,' she told him severely. 'Why didn't you wear something sensible? I want this table placed in the dead center of the room and all that paraphernalia over there carried across.'

The orderly murmured an apology. 'I didn't realize—' he began, but she brushed it aside. 'There's no time to waste!' she urged. 'The new pathologist will be here at any moment, and I want his table set out, ready and waiting.' She added to Nurse Warren: 'That, at least, will start me off on the right foot—I hope! You've got the test meal? Tell Sister Parker I'm sorry it wasn't down earlier.'

Bunny Warren paused beside the door and looked back. The theatre orderly—a fair-haired man with a distinct dash of red in his hair—was heaving the table across the room with astonishing strength. The only time they saw an orderly in the wards was when they brought the theatre trolley to bear a patient aloft. The girl thought vaguely that she had never seen this one before.

'I meant to tell you, Faith—I met Charity on the way up. She'll be late for supper tonight and wants you to tell Home Sister. She's massaging Matron's leg, and it has to be done after duty.'

Faith thanked her, adding: 'You'd better take the container in this enamel tray—' and handed one across. 'Sister will pounce if you dare to proffer it without!' She added a conspiratorial smile, then forgot about Nurse Warren as she turned her attention back to the orderly. Already the immense table was in position and the man was even maneuvering it directly beneath the lights. That was sensible, at least.

Nurse Warren closed the door and hurried back to the ward. Down there, in the ward kitchen, they'd all gather round, eager for a description of the new man. It was disappointing that she would be unable to supply it, but perhaps someone would be able to identify the new theatre orderly. He looked rather nice.

Back in the laboratory, Faith watched the man with equal interest. He looked a cut above the average orderly, she thought, and really quite intelligent. She said kindly: 'That's fine! Not even the new pathologist could complain at the way you've placed his table, I'm sure. Now if you'll just help me carry across his equipment—no, don't touch that microscope! Leave it to me—'

'It is too heavy for you.'

His voice was crisp and authoritative.

'Nonsense! I've been handling microscopes for four years.' Faith's voice was deliberately cool, for the man was regarding her with more interest than was fitting from a theatre orderly.

'Then you must have trained here,' the man said, 'since I should judge you to be in your very early twenties.'

She made no answer. She was embarking upon no personal conversation with him. His glance was too frank, too speculative. He had to be put in his place.

'That will be all,' she said. 'You may go now.'

'Go where?' he asked.

Startled, she looked at him. He even had the audacity to smile. His eyes twinkled in the most disconcerting fashion. Without doubt, he was too familiar, too confident. Without doubt, he had to be snubbed.

'Back to your work, of course. And thank Theatre Sister on my behalf for sending you. I appreciate it. You've been a great help. Now you may go.'

'But Theatre Sister did not send me,' the man said with infuriating calm.

It was then that the probing finger of fear touched her heart; a finger of apprehension and doubt. It was then that, in the remote recesses of her consciousness, she became vaguely uneasy. The man surely *was* an orderly? He couldn't be anyone else!

Nevertheless, her voice held a sharp edge of alarm as she said: 'Who are you? Where have you come from?'

A rap upon the door forestalled his answer. Faith called; 'Come in!' and a man wearing a green baize apron appeared upon the threshold. He said cheerfully: 'Sorry I'm late, miss—Sister couldn't spare me earlier . . .'

Faith went rigid. She could not speak. The man in the white coverall said: 'That's all right, Orderly. We've managed thank you,' and the man touched his forehead respectfully and departed. The door closed.

Faith swallowed—hard. Slowly, she turned and faced the man. He was smiling broadly, his shoulders shaking with suppressed laughter. Faith's hands flew to her cheeks covering their betraying flush. *Oh, horror!* she thought. She wanted to turn and run. She wanted to leap into a distant cupboard and hide. She could do neither. She had to stand here and face the man in the white coverall and put her hand into his extended one as he said: 'How do you do, Miss Connell? You are Miss Connell, I presume? Matron told me about you.' One eyebrow raised quizzically, as he finished: 'I don't think I need to introduce myself, do I?'

Faith gulped: 'No, Doctor Willstack—you don't!'

CHAPTER THREE

When Hope saw the new visiting surgeon for the first time, she thought spontaneously: He doesn't laugh enough! He has never learned to laugh! Why she thought thus, she had no idea. The man was tall and distinguished and utterly impersonal. He was well-known in the town, having made his mark during the past few years in no uncertain manner. As a surgeon, he was in great demand but, rumor had it, not everyone was fortunate enough to get him. Lady Ransom, rumor also said, had wanted him for one of her frequent operations, but the man had rejected her high fee with the frank comment that there was nothing whatever the matter with her.

If it were true—and Hope had no proof that it was —she admired the man for his courage. Not many people could stand up to the town's most influential inhabitant. Lady Ransom practically owned the whole of Highcliffe, and the part she didn't own just wasn't worth having.

Hope first saw Phillip Trent when he visited Luke's ward. There were three operations listed for the following day and, being newly arrived and therefore unacquainted with the cases, he wished to see the patients before they came to the theatre.

Little Nurse Warren threw one curious, apprehensive glance in the surgeon's direction and beat a hasty retreat to the ward kitchen. Even the conscientious student nurse, so eager to learn and even more eager to be noticed, found some menial job in the sluice and was glad of it. For Phillip Trent had the reverse effect from Hope Connell. He chilled, where she thawed; he rebuffed, where she encouraged; he rendered speechless where she invited confidence. The entire staff, from Sister down to the ward maids, were awed by him. The effect he would have upon the patients, thought Hope sadly, was alarming. They would be struck dumb, paralyzed with fear, or at least smitten with shyness.

Sister Parker was saying something in her precise, clipped voice, and Hope jerked her attention back to the moment.

'Numbers four, seven and ten are down for tomorrow morning's session, sir. The first is a common fracture—the Resident Surgeon will do that, of course. The second's an appendix and the third a laparotomy. The latter, of course, may take some time, but the appendix should be quite straightforward.'

'What age is the laparotomy case?'

'Sixty-five. And not very robust, I'm afraid. I'd say a high-strung type.' Sister Parker said it with a shade of irritation, and the surgeon cast her a shrewd and observant glance. A hard woman, he thought. Hard and very satisfied with herself. Why did women like this go in for nursing in the first place? The job needed a sympathetic nature and, above all, a heart. But so often one met women like Sister Parker in hospital wards—highly efficient, skilful, conscientious in the extreme, but completely lacking in understanding, intolerant of a patient's moral weakness.

He said abruptly: 'If she is nervous I'll see her first. After all, a laparotomy isn't a very pleasant thing to face, is it, Sister? I'd be more than apprehensive myself.'

'Only because you know what it means.'

'And this patient doesn't?'

'Of course not!'

'So she lies there, worrying and doubting and fearing the worst.'

Sister said tartly: 'You don't suggest that I should tell her the worst, do you, sir?'

'Sometimes,' he said slowly, 'it is wiser. Sometimes ignorance intensifies fear. It is amazing how frequently an apprehensive patient calms down when faced with the truth, I have never found human nature to be basically cowardly, Sister, despite all the theories.'

Sister Parker's lips tightened. The R.S.O. glanced sideways at Staff Nurse Connell, and raised significant eyebrows. This time Hope felt no annoyance with him, but complete agreement.

They reached the laparotomy bed—an old lady with a cloud of white hair and eyes as bright as berries. Right now they were bright with fear. 'I didn't sleep last night, Sister! Not a wink, I didn't . . .' Her voice quavered and died. Her hands, roughened with work, clutched the coverlet anxiously. Sister Parker said with cold and brisk efficiency: 'Nonsense, Mrs. Tompkins! You must have slept! Night Sister gave you a sedative, remember?'

The old lady looked mutinous.

'Didn't have no effect, it didn't.'

'Then we must ask Night Sister to give you something a little stronger tonight, mustn't we?'

'Don't like drugs, Sister. Don't hold with 'em.'

'But if you insist that you cannot sleep . . .'

Phillip Trent said quietly: 'Why can't you sleep, Mrs. Tompkins?' His voice was unexpectedly kind, and the woman's eyes slewed round to him in surprise. 'Something on your mind?' he asked, and although his serious face still did not smile, something in his voice made it easy for the old lady to do so.

Her tired mouth curved gratefully. 'Nurse knows why I can't sleep, don't you, Nurse?' She turned to Hope as to a friend. 'Ever so kind and understanding Nurse Connell is, sir.'

Sister's lips tightened. Staff Nurse Connell was much too friendly with the patients; too indulgent. Secretly, she resented Hope's popularity with them, although not for the world would she have admitted it, even to herself.

For the first time, the surgeon looked at the Staff Nurse. He saw a trim figure in white; a flame of copper-colored hair beneath a starched cap; immaculate bows beneath a pointed chin. And more. A pair of amber-brown eyes warmed by more than their color, eyes which looked back at the old lady and smiled encouragingly.

'In that case,' he said quietly, 'we must get Nurse Connell to tell us what the trouble is.'

Sister Parker's starched figure went rigid. She took it as a direct snub that he should discuss a patient's case with her subordinate in her own presence.

Stephen Barlow sensed Sister's reaction and checked a smile. His eyes sought Hope's again, but to his chagrin she was not looking at him at all. She was looking at the stern face of Phillip Trent and looking in a way Stephen did not like. Absorbed, interested, arrested.

He suppressed a sigh. Hope Connell was always so elusive, he thought ruefully. But one day—*one* day, he vowed—he would break down her indifference. He succeeded with other women. Why not with her?

Phillip Trent said briskly: 'Now, Nurse, tell me why Mrs. Tompkins cannot sleep.'

'She is worrying about her family, sir. She thinks they cannot manage without her.'

'That they can't, sir! I've never left 'em for a day!'

'So, of course,' said Hope seriously, 'she is afraid they aren't having proper meals and the house is being neglected and Mr. Tompkins' indigestion will start again.'

'He's a good man, sir—a kind one. But when his indigestion's on, well, he's not himself at all! So I do want to get home quick, to see he doesn't go eating fish'n' chips and fried stuff, what always brings it on.'

'Have you told him not to eat these things?' Phillip asked.

'Oh, of course, sir, but Fred's Daisy is supposed to be looking after him—going in to do the house and cook his meals when he can't get over to eat with them, and the only way to serve a meal that Daisy knows is out of a newspaper from the Handy Corner Fish Café down the street.'

'And who is Daisy?' Phillip Trent asked with interest—far too much interest, thought Sister Parker, who found a patient's relatives nothing but nuisances and considered that the less one heard about them, the better.

'My daughter-in-law, sir. A nice girl in her way, but not all our Fred thinks she is.'

'Have you any other children besides Fred, Mrs. Tompkins?'

The bright eyes softened with pride.

'That I have, sir. Four, all told. Alfred—he's farming in Canada and doing fine. And Ethel—the eldest girl, married, with two kids and lovely ones, too. Maud, what works in the Post Office, and Vi last of all. She's a shop assistant in Plymouth and only gets home week-ends, and what with Maud being out all day and Vi away all week, I has to rely on Daisy, sir. That's why I feel uneasy.'

Sister Parker suppressed her impatience. If Mr. Trent was going to waste so much time at every bedside, they wouldn't get through today! He made no attempt to control the old lady's rambling story, but listened with infinite patience as she continued with her family history. At the end of it he had a pretty complete picture of her background and her worries—and a lot more besides.

'Suppose,' he said gently, 'we ask the Almoner to check up on things, for you? Your husband comes to see you, doesn't he? I'll ask the Almoner to have a talk with him next time. If everything isn't absolutely right at home, she will find out, believe me. But it probably will be, you know. Your illness might be the making of young Daisy.'

'D'you think so, sir? I hope so, I'm sure.

She's always at me, saying I've done too much for Fred and his Dad . . .'

'Perhaps she is right. Anyway, we'll see what we can do to set your mind at rest—won't we, Nurse Connell?'

'Of course!' declared Hope, thinking how wrong she had been in her belief that this man would intimidate the patients; it was only upon the nursing staff that he had such an effect.

The old lady's eyes dimmed.

'You're very kind, I'm sure. But Mr. Tompkins is a proud man—he won't like confiding in a stranger.'

'He'll confide in us, I think,' Phillip said gently. 'We are looking after you, Mrs. Tompkins, so naturally anything which concerns you, concerns us. Remember that, won't you? It will help, I think. Remember it when you settle down tonight and I'm sure you will feel more at rest. It is very important that you sleep tonight you know. We're going to deal with this trouble of yours tomorrow morning.'

Mrs. Tompkins heaved a sigh of relief.

'Thank goodness for that, sir! I'll be glad when it's over and I can get back home. Will it be long before I can, sir?'

'That depends upon what I have to do.'

'Don't you know, sir?'

'I've a fair idea . . .'

'I heard Sister say I had a Lapper-something-or-other. What is it?'

'A laparotomy is the name we use for something we're a little uncertain of,' he said discreetly.

'Meaning you don't know what you're going to find, sir?'

'Meaning we're just going to take a look, to make sure. We'll probably get a pleasant surprise and find little or nothing, after all!'

And he actually smiled. Hope saw his stern mouth relax at the corners—compassionately, tenderly, with infinite solicitude.

And right at that moment, she fell in love with him.

Just like that, it happened. With no clash of cymbals, no roll of drums. There was nothing to herald the moment, nothing to prepare her, nothing to announce that this was a moment elevated above all others and, therefore, to be held captive and marveled over. It came in the middle of a crowded morning—illogically, a little ridiculously, for the man was a stranger, and a forbidding stranger, at that. Nevertheless, it happened, catching her unawares and leaving her breathless and a little afraid.

She heard, as from a distance, the old lady's voice saying tiredly: 'Well, it's all a bit of a nuisance, isn't it, sir?' She gave a wry chuckle. 'I must say, I hope you find *something* for your trouble! Seems a waste of time otherwise, don't it?' Her valiant old mouth quivered slightly. 'Will Nurse Connell be there with me?' she asked hopefully.

Sister Parker put in briskly: 'Staff Nurse will be on duty in the wards, Mrs. Tompkins.'

The frail voice quavered. 'I'm sorry to hear that. I kind've hoped you'd be with me, Nurse. I wouldn't be so scared then, and I expect I will be scared when the time comes, won't I? I'm not now, I must admit. Too tired, somehow . . .'

'Nor will you be then, Mrs. Tompkins,' Phillip Trent promised, 'because you'll be asleep. We'll see to that. But if it makes you any happier to have Nurse Connell with you, I'm sure we can arrange it, can't we, Sister?'

He said it in a tone which brooked no denial. If his most serious case needed humoring, then, said his voice, she should be humored. Sister Parker admitted grudgingly that she supposed it could be arranged.

The surgeon turned back to the old lady and said gently: 'Nurse Connell will be with you, Mrs. Tompkins—I promise you that. We'll take care of you together, she and I . . .'

CHAPTER FOUR

On his way to Mark's ward, Phillip Trent passed the private room occupied by Caroline Ransom. A nurse was just coming out, and through the open door he glimpsed the flower-bedecked room, and, in the midst of it, enthroned upon her pillows, Caroline herself.

The house physician was with her. Phillip caught the door before it closed and thrust his head inside. 'Hello, Shearing—so you've arrived.'

He held out his hand. He had known Mike Shearing since boyhood and knew his history; knew his upbringing and his bitterness, his character and ability. Of the last two qualities he thought highly, but his upbringing and its effects he deplored. All the same, he liked Michael; had always done so. It was partly due to his persuasion that the boy had applied for the post at St. Bede's, and, to Phillip's gratification had been appointed.

He was gratified for two reasons; first, because Michael had been determined to get away from Highcliffe ('Why shouldn't I? I've no bond of affection for the place!') and, second, because they would be working in the same hospital together—Michael full time, himself as visiting surgeon. Thus he would be able to keep his eye on him.

Caroline Ransom looked at him archly. 'Come in, Phillip!' she called. 'How lovely to see you! I was delighted to hear you were appointed, especially since you got Mummy's back up!'

She held out an exquisitely manicured hand. Lying there with nothing more serious than a muscular injury, she had hours to spare beautifying herself, and, thought Phillip wryly, appeared to be making the most of it. A lavish make-up box stood open beside her bed. Numerous glass-stoppered bottles containing colored liquids—nail varnishes, he presumed—surrounded it. There were cigarettes and chocolates, fruits and magazines.

'What is all this?' he asked, taking her hand. 'A branch of Selfridge's?'

Her laugh was high-pitched and affected. She adored Phillip Trent's frankness. 'It's the brute force of the man,' she confided to her friends. 'Such a change from the rest of Highcliffe's social set!' But there was something else about him, too—a reserve, a self-sufficiency, a complete indifference to her. These things challenged her. To a girl who had just 'come out,' a successful man in his thirties held a distinct appeal.

She smiled up at him in a way she considered irresistible.

'You seem to be having a very luxurious time,' he said dryly. 'This place reeks to high heaven! Why don't you send some of these flowers out to the main ward? There are patients there, I'm sure, who get little or nothing. One old lady I've just been talking to down in Luke's would be thrilled by just one of these roses.'

'She shall have the lot!' Caroline cried, in just the way her mother would have made a magnificent gesture, but if it impressed

Michael Shearing, it failed utterly with the older man.

'She won't want the lot,' he answered. 'Shower her with flowers and the poor dear might think we anticipate her funeral!' Caroline trilled her appreciation and Phillip, turning toward the door, finished; 'If you can really spare a few, however, ask one of the nurses to take them down to Mrs. Tompkins, in Luke's. Bed number ten.'

'I'll do that,' Caroline promised, 'and Phillip—don't go! I do so want to ask if it is really true, what you told Mummy? I can scarcely believe it, but you seem to have got her back up so much that I'm sure you must have said something outrageous! What was it, Phillip?'

He looked back at her. He saw her mother's calculating glance, her mother's vain assurance. The child thought she was irresistible; what she really needed was a good spanking—something her mother had never had, and could certainly have benefited from. He glanced across at Michael and saw the frown of impatience between the young man's level brows. He wanted to get on with his work, resenting any hindrance. But was that the only reason for his irritation?

'Anything wrong?' he asked.

'Nothing I can't deal with, sir.'

Instantly forgetting her question, Caroline Ransom said eagerly: 'And you *will* deal with it, won't you, Doctor? I mean, it's too ridiculous that I should have to go all the way up to the physiotherapist's room when she could perfectly well come to me! She *should* come to me. After all, I'm a private patient.'

All this, thought Phillip thankfully, had nothing to do with him. His hand had actually reached the door knob and turned it when Michael's answer arrested him.

'I will speak to Miss Connell myself.'

'Connell?' echoed Phillip. 'Do you mean Nurse Connell, the staff nurse in Luke's? She seemed a very capable girl, to me. Is it she who insists that you go to the therapist for treatment? How can she—she isn't nursing you, is she?' Phillip could not understand why he was so interested in Staff Nurse Connell, or why he should be disturbed by a vague feeling of resentment at the idea of Caroline Ransom criticizing her.

It seemed, however, that he was wrong, for Caroline shook her golden head, and the fan of her hair, smooth and shining and beautiful, swayed like a curtain about her shoulders. She was wearing a yellow ostrich feather bed jacket which, thought Phillip, made her look like an Easter chicken.

'Oh no,' she said, 'I mean the other one—her sister, I believe. She does massage and things like that. She came down here to give me my first treatment, but now she says she prefers that I should go to her.'

'And does it hurt you to do so? Surely not! You are transported there, I presume?'

Caroline evaded that. She pouted charmingly and said: 'That's hardly the point!'

'I'll take the matter up with her right away,' Michael promised, and followed Phillip Trent from the room.

* * *

Charity was alone when Michael entered. She had just finished massaging a patient and, with meticulous care, was changing the white sheet upon the high couch. She turned at the sound of his footsteps and stood waiting.

'Don't let me interrupt,' he said briskly, and at once she continued with her work, moving in her gentle, rather precise way. Her movements were graceful and unhurried, and he stood for a while, watching her. He had never seen anyone move quite as she did. He had no idea why he was so interested.

After a moment she said: 'I presume you have come to see me about something, Doctor?'

'I have indeed. A patient of mine. Miss Ransom.'

Charity's hands, folding towels, were immediately still.

'What about Miss Ransom?'

'I want to know why it is necessary for her to come up here for treatment.'

'It isn't absolutely necessary,' Charity answered carefully. 'Just preferable.'

'But why? You are more capable of moving about than she.'

He saw her mouth flicker in a smile. It was a lovely mouth—gently curved and sweet. The kind of mouth, he thought savagely, against which a man steeled himself. These gentle women were always deceptive.

'A nurse can bring her, Doctor. She can be wheeled in a hospital chair, and brought up by elevator.'

'You can go down by elevator, and transport yourself without the aid of a chair.'

'I can,' she admitted, and again the shadow of a smile played about her mouth; a teasing little smile. She wasn't taking him seriously, he felt, and that infuriated him.

'Then I suggest you do!' he retorted angrily.

'I am perfectly willing to,' she answered with maddening calm, 'but I am surprised to hear that Miss Ransom wants me to. After the last treatment she seemed only too eager to visit me instead. Which was only natural, in the circumstances.'

Against his will, he said: 'What circumstances?'

'Unfortunately, I overturned a vase of flowers, Doctor. They were at her bedside. Here there are no vases to get in the way; nothing to represent any danger.'

'Surely you could keep your eyes open for

such things, and avoid them? Better still, have them removed beforehand!'

He was being rude, and he knew it. He did not care. She had been rude to him when first they met, ignoring his outstretched hand, refusing to extend even that courtesy to him. From that moment on he had wanted to retaliate.

She answered quietly: 'I would if I saw them, of course. Unfortunately, Doctor, I cannot.'

He said, checking swift alarm: 'What do you mean?'

'Simply what I say.' She smiled again, this time openly and with pleasure. 'You have paid me the greatest compliment in the world, Doctor Shearing, if you really and truly have not realized that I am blind.'

CHAPTER FIVE

Across the wide courtyard which separated the nurses' home from the main hospital block, Faith could see the frosted glass window of the laboratory. Behind it shone a clear fluorescent light, with the silhouetted figure of a man stooping above a table. The man, of course, was Charles Willstack, and despite the fact that official working hours were over, he was still hard at it over there—determined, apparently, to become *au fait* as quickly as possible with everything in hand.

Faith stood at the open window of her bedroom and looked across the dividing space, watching the bent figure thoughtfully. This was the hour when the day staff came off duty and the night staff took over. Dusk was enfolding the courtyard like an old lady's cloak. It was an hour she usually enjoyed, when the pulse of hospital life changed; an enchanted hour, marking the transition from day to night. Vaguely she was aware of night nurses hurrying across to the wards, their dark capes swinging, their knitting and magazines, customary equipment for a long vigil, tucked beneath their arms. But tonight she saw none of them with active awareness; they were merely background shadows accompanying, and emphasizing, her thoughts. And these thoughts were centered exclusively upon young Doctor Willstack.

Hope's voice, from behind, cut into her meditation.

'What interests you outside? You seem very preoccupied, Faith.'

'Oh—nothing!' Faith answered vaguely. She added, to change the subject: 'I wonder what time Charity will be through . . .'

'She should be back by now. Mustard has gone to meet her.'

'Yes—I can see him, sitting down there by the staff entrance. I shan't bother to go down for a meal until she comes. Home Sister is keeping it for us.'

'Good. I'll wait, too. This is to be an odd job night for me, and then early to bed. I'm doing theatre duty in the morning.'

That brought Faith round in surprise. She turned her back upon the window and upon that distant, silhouetted figure.

'Theatre duty?' she echoed in surprise. 'How come?'

'The new surgeon arranged it. Old Mrs. Tompkins—I told you about her.'

'The laparotomy? What do you think they'll find, Hope?'

'Cancer, I'm afraid. How bad, we don't know. Poor darling—she's the sweetest thing; always thinking of her family, never of herself.'

Hope, her copper hair piled high, her slim figure wrapped in a shabby old dressing-gown, was wiping cream from her face with a tissue. In her own mirror she observed her sister across the room. Faith seemed unusually absorbed this evening. Of course, she was always serious, but tonight she seemed even more so.

Faith, who had turned back to the window and her private thoughts, now jerked to awareness again.

'Charity is coming now,' she said. 'Mustard knows.'

Down in the dim shadows of the courtyard, the lively figure of the blind girl's dog sprang to its feet. Each evening, on the stroke of six, he posted himself at the staff exit of the hospital block, waiting for his mistress. When she was late, as tonight, he simply lay down and waited for her. She would come; he always knew she would come. More than that, he sensed precisely when she was coming, rising quietly to welcome her, thrusting his cold nose into the palm of her hand in greeting; never rushing her, never leaping exuberantly against her, never startling her. His devotion was deep and unfailing. He was her guide and friend.

Faith smiled gently. Hope came and stood beside her and, together, they watched their sister's progress across the courtyard. An ambulance whirled through the gates, its light flashing, and at once Mustard pressed against his mistress' side and she obeyed, standing still and waiting until, at his signal, the way was clear for them to cross. Unaware of her sisters' vigil above, Charity approached. They never rushed to meet her, never treated her as anything but physically normal, for, apart from her lack of sight, she was healthy and full of life and extremely independent.

'She's lovely,' Faith said softly. 'What a pity she cannot see how lovely!'

'Perhaps that is what makes her so—complete unconsciousness of self.'

Affectionately, they watched her until she was lost in the shadows immediately below. A few moments later they heard her tread upon the short flight of stairs which led straight up to their room. Home Sister had arranged it thus when they came to live at the nurses' home, giving them a room which they could share. On the floors above the rest of the nurses had single rooms, little more than cubicles, but none of them begrudged the Connell sisters their roomy accommodation, for this room represented their home; they had no other to visit in off-duty hours; none but Matron's quarters over in the hospital where, of course, they were always welcome. Apart from that, this room with the three iron bedsteads represented their own private kingdom.

It was an easy flight of stairs for Charity to negotiate; ten steps in all, which she knew by heart. The second, fourth and seventh all creaked; outside the door of their room was a loose floor board which creaked, also. She knew then that she was home. The door knob was just slightly above the level of her right hand.

Within the room was less austerity than the bare, linoleumed staircase. A carpet, which they had bought out of their combined earnings; an easy chair beside each bed; personal items belonging to their parents which gave to the place a feeling of home. Each of them loved this room and, for Charity's sake, no piece of furniture was ever moved. Mustard abandoned his vigilance once he delivered his mistress at the door. He lived downstairs, in comfortable quarters just off the kitchen, but Sister turned a blind eye when, as now, he entered the girls' room and settled down comfortably before the radiator.

When Charity appeared, Hope was back at her dressing table and Faith at her wardrobe.

Hope pinned her hair high, gathered up her soap and towels and sang merrily: 'My turn to be first in the bathroom! Sorry, girls!'

'Don't use all the hot water!' Charity warned. 'I want to wash my hair tonight. It feels awful!'

'Want me to set it?' Faith asked, discarding her frock and donning a housecoat of striped taffeta. Charity heard its familiar rustle. That meant that Faith was settling down to an evening at home.

'If you've time. I gather you're not going out?'

'No. There's a program I want to listen to. If we don't waste time over supper, we can get back up here in time to listen in peace. There's always such a babel down in the assembly room. I'll set your hair while the concert's on.'

'Lovely! What's the program?'

'Chopin, Grieg, and Mendelssohn. Changing into anything, Charity?'

'My old green housecoat, I think. I usually wear that when washing my hair. It's so old it doesn't matter!'

Faith made no attempt to fetch it for her.

Charity selected the housecoat herself, by touch. She knew exactly where her wardrobe stood, just where the handle was, and the precise position of the garment —third hanger from the left. She knew the feel of the material, also; warm and comfortable. The whole evening, she thought contentedly, promised to be warm and comfortable.

And so it was, for all three of them. Mending; hair-washing; music and gossip. At ten o'clock they prepared for bed. By that time they had discussed the day's events; problem cases; Sister Parker's temper; Matron's bad knee. As they settled down for the night, Hope asked sleepily: 'And what is the new pathologist like, Faith?'

To her surprise, her sister hesitated.

'Frankly, I don't know,' she said after a moment.

'You don't know! Why? Hasn't he arrived?'

'Oh, yes—he has arrived. With a vengeance! The lab doesn't seem like the same place. He's like a tornado, rushing through it; revolutionizing it; changing everything.'

'What has he changed?'

'Well—nothing, yet. But I've a horrible feeling he is going to! He's so *different* . . .'

'From Doctor Walker, you mean?' Charity asked, climbing into bed. 'In what way?'

'Young, for one thing. Surprisingly young. No more than thirty-ish, I'm sure. He hasn't Doctor Walker's dignity, at all.'

'Do you expect it, at his age? Old Walker was nearly seventy,' Hope pointed out.

She was right, of course. All the same, serious-minded Faith could not bring herself to approve of the new pathologist.

'He's too friendly,' she said.

'And isn't that a good thing?'

'I'm not sure.'

'Perhaps that is because you are unaccustomed to it in that stuffy old lab!' Charity laughed.

Faith wondered if she was right. Charity was so often right. Doctor Walker had been leisurely, slow, kindly and pompous; very conscious of his position and determined that his staff should be. All the same, they had loved him. In contrast, Doctor Willstack was buoyant, brisk, and determined.

'Do you like him?' Hope asked.

Again Faith hesitated. When she spoke she did so abruptly, almost defiantly. 'No,' she answered, remembering her anger with him, her fury that he should trick her, her humiliation because he had laughed at her appalling mistake. Faith was sensitive and shy; to start an acquaintanceship on such a footing was embarrassing enough, but that such an acquaintanceship should be a professional one, and therefore important, made matters worse.

The whole thing was disturbing. The man himself was disturbing. His eloquent eyes were disturbing; his smile, his voice, his laughter—all were disturbing.

She changed the subject abruptly.

'What about the new surgeon? Have you seen him?'

'Yes. He came to Luke's this afternoon; wanted to see tomorrow's cases. He's operating on old Mrs. Tompkins at eleven.' Hope paused. 'It was he who arranged theatre duty for me, so that I could be with her.'

Charity said: 'That was a nice thing to do. Did he realize she was your favorite patient?'

'She isn't my favorite—I'm just naturally anxious about her, that's all.'

Behind the dark screen of her eyes, Charity smiled. Hope never liked to reveal her tender heart —but her patients saw it. Her sisters saw it.

Faith smiled, too. 'What is he like, as a man?' she asked.

Hope's heart skipped a beat. Even to think of him awakened that disturbing reaction which had caught her unawares this afternoon. It left her breathless and excited and a little frightened. Not even her professional self-control could quite eliminate a tremor in her voice as she answered: 'What is he like? Stern and forbidding and unapproachable . . . keen on his work . . . interested in his patients. Tall. Prematurely grey at the temples. A good voice —crisp and deep. I suppose one would call him "distinguished." '

Faith raised her eyebrows expressively. They were well-defined eyebrows, naturally arched, but she was quite unaware of their beauty, as she was unaware of most things about herself. She was also unaware that the new pathologist had noticed them at first glance, and that his appreciation had included her serious, sensitive face.

Charles Willstack was an observant man. In the vast London hospital which he had just left, there had been many pretty girls and he had enjoyed himself with most of them; here, in this little Devonian town, was a girl of a vastly different type, a girl who was to work as his right hand and one, he judged, who would prove difficult to know; one who erected barriers and retired behind them. Shy, reserved, sensitive. It might take him quite a time, he thought, to break down those barriers, but he would do it in the end.

But of this, also, Faith was unaware. Listening to her sister's description of the new surgeon, she forgot the new pathologist.

'You noticed a lot about him, in so short a time,' she commented with gentle amusement.

'Nonsense!' declared Hope. And she, too, shied away from the subject, turning inevitably to the third and last.

'Has either of you seen the new house physician?' she asked.

'Not I,' said Faith. 'He's visiting the path. lab. tomorrow morning at ten. He rang this afternoon, asking if he might. He has a nice voice.'

'But an angry one,' Charity put in quietly.

'Angry?' echoed Hope. 'Why angry?'

'I don't know. But at some time in his life something has happened to Doctor Shearing, something that hurt him. And he is still hitting out against it.'

The sisters looked across at the third bed. Charity's serene face was full of pity. Was it her blindness, they wondered, which made her capable of seeing below the surface of people's minds?

'The story has gone around the hospital that he's thoroughly objectionable and ill-mannered,' Hope said. 'Bunny Warren told me.'

'He gives that impression,' Charity agreed, and said no more.

CHAPTER SIX

Entering Matthew's ward in the wake of his senior officer, Michael's eyes flew to the woman in bed number seven. She looked no different—pallid, weary, listless. Upon examination her condition was unchanged, which brought a frown to the senior physician's eyes. He was beginning to get perturbed about this patient, but was unwilling to admit it. There was nothing to do—he agreed with Sister—but continue the treatment as before. The shortness of breath, the irregular heart action—both must be steadied, both checked carefully.

He felt frustrated by the patient's lack of response and, once outside the ward, admitted it. 'It is almost as if she doesn't *want* to respond!' he said impatiently, and Sister Matthew shook her head in agreement. That, she said, must be the explanation. With a patient like that, one sometimes fought a losing battle.

A sound from the new house physician brought his senior's eyes round to him; a sound of dissension, of protest; a spontaneous sound which could not be checked.

'Well,' rapped Stacey, 'what were you going to say, Shearing?'

'I merely wanted to ask a question, sir.'

The answer was respectful, but without docility. Young Doctor Shearing, thought his chief, would never become the docile type—and a good thing, too. He'd have been irritated by him, if so.

'Well?' he said again, and waited.

'I wondered whether the patient's lymphatic glands might be impaired or affected.'

Ward Sister raised astonished eyebrows. 'Really,' they said, 'whatever next—from a subordinate doctor to his chief, too!' But Stacey looked at him shrewdly for a long moment, said nothing, and walked on. Nor did he speak to Michael again on the subject of patient number seven on Matthew's ward.

Michael subsided, and, feeling vaguely resentful, determined to pass no comments whatsoever in future, unless asked. But he was a man of impulses; frank, outspoken, too antagonistic toward the world to become meek and quiescent. For the rest of the morning, however, the Senior Physician was troubled no more by suggestions from his subordinate, a fact which, had Michael realized it, rather disappointed Stacey. Although he had made no answer, young Doctor Shearing's question had impressed him. It showed, at least, that the fellow used his brains.

Speculating upon his observation, Doctor Stacey proceeded to Luke's ward, where Staff Nurse Connell conducted them briskly on their round, finally excusing herself as soon as a relief nurse appeared, explaining that she was due for theatre duty herself.

Doctor Stacey raised surprised eyebrows. 'How come?' he asked.

'Old Mrs. Tompkins—the laparotomy,' Hope explained. 'Mr. Trent thinks she should be indulged.'

'And she wants you with her?' The senior physician smiled. 'That won't please Sister, will it? I imagine she doesn't like her routine interfered with.'

Hope assumed an expression of tactful

ignorance. 'I've no idea, Doctor,' she said meekly, and departed—but not before Michael glimpsed the dimple which trembled at the corner of her mouth. It was so astonishingly like the blind physiotherapist's that he recognized their relationship at once. He glanced at Hope's retreating back with interest. So this, he thought, is another of the trio . . . Apart from the fact that she walked more briskly than Charity, their movements were very similar.

For some indefinable reason Michael was sorry when Hope Connell disappeared for, in an equally indefinable way, she had soothed his resentment, and because he was a young man with a questing mind he sought for the reason, and found it. She had soothed him only from the moment that he recognized her identity—and so recalled the serene young woman with hair the color of ripe corn and sightless eyes which looked upon the world as if seeing her own vision of it, and finding it beautiful.

The recollection of Charity's quiet repose was like a benediction, soothing his stormy mind, calming his resentment. Even so had she lurked in the deep recesses of his consciousness ever since their first moment of meeting, and more actively so since their conversation together. He wondered now whether he had given his attention so determinedly to the patient in Matthew's ward as a means of escape, and in a desire to suppress his reaction to Charity Connell. He was disturbed to think that this might be so, for no girl had ever touched the secret places of his heart before, and if it was necessary for him to seek forgetfulness of her in work, then Charity had indeed penetrated deep.

Speculating thus, Michael followed the senior physician to the private wards, and the first they entered was Caroline Ransom's. As before, she looked very entrancing, decked in a fluffy angora bed jacket of softest pink—like an outsize powderpuff. Seated beside her bed was an elegant young woman. She wore a beautifully cut suit of moss green, with a lavish mink stole and a chic little moss green hat trimmed with mink tails. Her whole appearance was costly and precious and she was certainly beautiful, lacking Caroline's effusive girlishness. She was *soignée* and poised and extremely sophisticated. She was also, thought Michael shrewdly, extremely brittle, extremely hard, and extremely determined.

The senior physician's eyebrows rose. 'Visiting hours so early in the day?' he asked pointedly, and the elegant young woman uttered a trilling laugh and answered serenely: 'I inveigled Sister into admitting me!' She refrained to add how responsive was embittered Sister Parker to a bottle of Chanel No. 5. Instead she tilted a provocative eyebrow and asked archly: 'Any objections, Doctor?'

'Only that I want to examine your sister.'

'Meaning you want me to go?'

'Meaning something like that,' smiled Doctor Stacey, who was by no means unsusceptible.

Felicity Drake rose with leisurely ease. She was bored, anyway, and only too glad to get away from Caroline's prattle. Caroline irritated her. She was spoiled and wilful and far too inquisitive—especially regarding herself and Phillip Trent. She also had the uncomfortable knack of putting her finger right on the truth at times; this, of course, was because she possessed a one-track mind, and at present that mind revolved upon one subject only—men. Therefore she had seen right through Felicity's reason for calling this morning. Not for one moment had Caroline swallowed the excuse about bringing her clean laundry which could have been sent direct from home. The maddening chit had looked at her pertly and said: 'You're a bit early, aren't you, Felicity? Phillip isn't due in the theatre until ten. I know, because one of the nurses told me.' And when Felicity calmly seated herself and crossed one elegant leg over the other, her young sister continued with brutal directness: 'Oh, I see—you mean to hang around. Time your exit for nine-forty-five, Felicity, and you should meet him in the hall.'

There was no love between the sisters. Caroline envied the freedom which marriage and a divorce had given Felicity, and Felicity was—although, as yet, she refused to admit it—beginning to envy her younger sister's youth and freshness. Right at this moment it did little to foster affection to realize that Caroline touched a focal point of truth when attributing her visit to a desire to see Phillip Trent.

But in the presence of the two doctors (and who *was* that handsome young scowling one?) Felicity made a great display of sisterly affection, kissing Caroline tenderly upon the cheek and urging her to 'Get well soon, darling! We are all so *worried* about you!' She skilfully evaded Caroline's skeptical glance, turned the full tilt of a radiant smile upon Doctor Stacey, inclined her elegant head toward the saturnine young man, and departed.

This, it seemed, was her lucky day, for as she emerged Phillip was stepping out of his car. He turned to give some direction to Hibbs, his chauffeur-valet, then leaped up the wide stone steps, two at a time. At the top he pulled up abruptly, for his way was barred by Felicity's elegant figure.

She laid a hand upon his sleeve—a hand encased in a long glove of moss-green suede, and murmured his name caressingly. 'Phillip!' It was a gentle murmur of affectionate reproach. 'Darling, have you been so frightfully busy that you haven't had time to ring me for the past week?'

'Frightfully,' he agreed, and smiled down into her upturned face. It was a characteristic smile—brief, touching only the corners of his mouth, conveying little amusement or even enjoyment. She thought, as she thought so often, that his sternness, far from being intimidating, was exciting. She liked a challenge, and reserve such as his was enough to challenge any woman. Conquest was always more satisfying if achieved against odds.

She let her suede-covered hand slip into the crook of his arm.

'Dinner tonight?' she murmured. 'It's a long time since you let me demonstrate my prowess as a cook!'

She had it all planned. A delectable meal exquisitely served; fragile china and gleaming silver; snowy linen and perfect wines. And, of course, candlelight. Candlelight gleaming upon rich mahogany; candlelight reflected in beautiful brocades; candlelight flattering her own carefully nurtured beauty. In candlelight lay romance.

He said, in that deep, crisp voice of his: 'My dear, I'm so sorry—I've a lecture at eight-thirty at the University.'

She hid her disappointment well.

'Then why not come later?'

'Because I've no idea how late I shall be. These students have alert minds—sometimes their questions run on indefinitely.'

She pouted prettily.

'The chairman should set a time limit for questions.'

'He usually does, but it makes no difference. I dare say I'm as much to blame as the students—I like answering their questions, especially if they are provocative and lead to debate.'

She was wise enough not to persist. Nevertheless, she turned with him into the main hall, her arm still linked in his. A nurse with a vivid flame of hair gleaming beneath a crisp cap was walking toward the staff elevator. She paused with her finger upon the button, looking back at them. Felicity was accustomed to people's stares and, therefore, paid no heed. But Phillip did. Just why he stiffened, he had no idea. Nor had Felicity, but she felt the tension of his arm beneath her own.

'Tomorrow, then, Phillip? It's the Hunt Ball and you're joining our party—remember?'

He jerked to attention. The red-haired nurse was opening the elevator gates, stepping inside, closing them again. The little cage slid upward and vanished, and the busy main hall seemed suddenly empty.

'I won't forget, Felicity. It was nice of your mother to invite me.' Again his stern mouth tilted at the corners. 'Especially under the circumstances,' he said.

Felicity threw back her lovely head and laughed.

'Dance with her, darling—but only once, or I shall be madly jealous!—and she'll forgive you. Actually, of course, you were right to be frank with her. Mother is too wrapped up in her imaginary ailments, and you're the only medico who has ever had the courage to tell her so.'

'It wasn't courage,' said Phillip; 'it was the truth. A man as busy as I is compelled to tell the truth—'

'—when persistent women want to engage him for unnecessary operations,' Felicity finished for him. 'I know, Phillip—and I quite agree with you, of course. Why *should* Mother be pandered to? She panders to herself too much.'

She released his arm reluctantly.

'Then I shan't see you before tomorrow night, Phillip?'

'My dear, I'm sorry—'

And he was. There were moments when Felicity disturbed him, and this was one of those moments. Despite his reserve, he had always been most potently aware of her. A man, he thought, would have to be a pretty cold sort of fish not to respond to such appeal, not to appreciate such beauty. As a boy he had stood in awe of her, aware that he had little to offer a daughter of the gods. He wasn't surprised when a man like Marcus Drake won her—nor, in a secret corner of his mind, was he surprised when the marriage fell through.

Felicity, he always felt, would have been a different person if not born to wealth, but despite his perception, despite his awareness of her faults, he had been, and still was, most potently disturbed by her.

Her heart trembled. Sensing his response, she took advantage of it to say: 'I could drive you home from the lecture, Phillip. You'll be tired after it, I'm sure.'

'Hibbs is collecting me,' he said, to her acute disappointment.

'Then put him off! Give the poor man a free evening for once!'

He laughed wryly.

'You ought to try putting Hibbs off, Felicity! He's the most tenacious fellow. Do you know what he does on these occasions? Slips into the back of the hall—and sits through the whole thing. Says he enjoys it. I can't think why.'

'I can. I'd enjoy it, too. Oh, yes, I would! I'm not the feather-brain you think me, Phillip.'

'I don't think you anything of the sort. You're an intelligent woman, Felicity, I know that. But to-night's lecture would bore you unutterably.' Gently, he disengaged her hand. 'I must go,' he said. 'I'm due in the theatre—'

He broke off abruptly, surprise showing in his eyes. Felicity followed his glance. There stood the red-haired nurse again. 'Excuse me, sir,' she said politely, 'but Theatre Sister sent me down to check on your arrival . . .'

'Tell her I'll be right up, Nurse.'

'I will, sir.'

She departed briskly, but not before her deep-set eyes had met Felicity's, fair and square, leaving an inexplicable sense of alarm in the older woman's self-centered heart. But was it really alarm? Felicity wondered. If so, why? The girl was nothing but a creature in uniform. A stiff apron and a starched collar; flat heels and an unbecoming frock—that was all she was.

Phillip said abruptly: 'Goodbye, my dear—' and at once became Phillip Trent the surgeon; detached, impersonal, remote.

Felicity watched his retreating back with anger and resentment and a blinding jealousy.

CHAPTER SEVEN

Entering the pathological laboratory, Michael pulled up abruptly. He was looking across the room at Charity's profile, and the sight of it was profoundly disturbing. It was almost uncanny, too—like coming face to face with her in unexpected places. When the profile turned and regarded him, he saw Charity's features with only a slight variation, but crowned by hair as dark and glossy as a black tulip. Deep blue eyes looked at him—serious and intent and, right at this moment, inquiring.

To his own surprise, he said: 'You must be

the third Miss Connell.'

Faith smiled spontaneously, and immediately her serious face was transformed. Not only Michael observed the transformation, but the chief pathologist also, straightening up from his intent scrutiny through a microscope. Briefly, Charles Willstack was still. He was wishing that she would retain that smile, or produce it more often. It revealed teeth as white and opalescent as pearls, softly curving lips, and an expression so radiant that it was like sunlight piercing the room. When smiling, Faith Connell was beautiful. When unsmiling, she was merely a shadow of her true self.

She said: 'Yes, I am the third Miss Connell. You must be Doctor Shearing. My sister told me about you—'

She broke off abruptly. Now why, she wondered, did I say that? Charity said so little about him—and yet so much. In her very silence had been significance, making her sisters aware of the new house physician—or aware that *she* had been aware of him . . .

Mike Shearing said: 'Indeed?' and wondered which sister she referred to. It could, of course, only be Charity, since he had not met the other until this morning—and then exchanged hardly a word. He felt a surprised sort of trembling in his heart and a compelling desire to ask the third Miss Connell just what the first one had said about him. Shyness, however, overcame him, and the next moment there was Doctor Willstack, hand outstretched, coming toward him and saying: 'So you made it, after all? Finished your round early? Good. Come right in and have a look around.'

Immediately, Michael felt at ease.

* * *

The operating theatre was ready. The trolley with its neat array of shining drums; the lotion bowls and steaming tray of instruments; the hissing sterilizer and the shadowless lights; the table, clean and expectant and waiting . . .

The fracture had been set by Stephen Barlow, and now he grumbled because he was not allocated the next job. Not that he deceived the nurses one whit; they all knew perfectly well that he was only too willing to hand over his responsibilities to any convenient hand. Why he went in for surgery, Hope often wondered. 'You should have had a nice cushy job in a Government office,' she had once told him, 'drinking cups of tea with one eye on the clock.' She had said it good-naturedly, but she'd meant it all the same. To Stephen a job was merely a means of earning a living; he had chosen medicine because it was in his family tradition and he could think of no alternative. Or so he said.

Sister Theatre glanced approvingly round the theatre; the mess caused by the fracture setting had been skilfully erased and now they were all ready for the appendix. 'Spinal anaesthetic,' she ordered briefly. 'Everything ready, Nurse?'

'Everything, Sister.'

The door opened and Phillip entered, nodding briefly to Sister Theatre. 'Ready in a moment,' he told her, and hurried to the scrubbing-up room. He was annoyed with Felicity for detaining him, but even more annoyed with himself for allowing her to. After all, bless her, how was she to appreciate the importance of hospital routine—especially theatre routine?

Meticulously he scrubbed his hands, his wrists, his forearms, his elbows. Dexterously, a nurse smeared his dripping hands with sterilized glycerine, then rolled on his rubber gloves. Swiftly, neatly, she wrapped his voluminous apron around him; tied his mask. The door dividing the scrubbing-up room from the theatre opened briefly, and Sister Theatre's voice called: 'Patient is ready, sir!'

Phillip nodded and, upon rubber-shod feet, strode into the humid room. Condensation streamed upon the vast windows; the tiled walls and floor had been hosed down by a theatre orderly. The whole process of preparation was swift and methodical and accurately timed. Beside the table stood the resident surgical officer, who was to assist him, and beside the instrument trolley stood Sister

Theatre, her forceps at the ready. The appendix was straightforward and simple. He left the stitching-up to his assistant and went back into the scrubbing-up room again, shedding his apron and his mask, starting the whole cleansing process once more.

It was not until the laparotomy came up that Phillip realized the identity of the theatre nurse. It was the little red-headed girl from Luke's ward—the girl the patient had wanted beside her. Her bright hair was concealed beneath a tightly swathed cap, but her lovely amber-colored eyes were revealed above her surgical mask. Swathed in an ample theatre apron, her hands rubber-shod, her small feet rubber-booted, there was nothing but those eyes to reveal any personality about the mummy-like figure. She moved lightly and carefully; well-trained and efficient. But the eyes were not the eyes of a machine-like figure; they were alive and vital and strangely disturbing. He was aware of them as he would have been aware of the warm comfort of a fire, sustaining him.

He returned to the theatre just as the anaesthetist trundled in his machine and began to fiddle with its cogs and wheels. Old Mrs. Tompkins, already drowsy from the injection given her down on the ward, was inquiring hopefully for Nurse Connell. 'I'm here, dear,' said Hope gently, stooping above her. Sister Theatre said: 'You'd better let her see your face, Nurse—just to reassure her.' Hope pulled down her mask briefly, revealing all the tenderness and concern she felt for the old lady. Mrs. Tompkins's eyes smiled . . . closed . . . slept. She was content, and quite unafraid, for Nurse Connell was with her . . . Nurse Connell would look after her . . .

Theatre Sister smiled behind her mask and said: 'She's certainly pinning her faith on you, Nurse!' Phillip couldn't see Hope's face now, but he knew that she, too, smiled. He knew more than that. He knew just *how* she smiled—with infinite tenderness —and some deep instinct told him that she smiled despite her fear. He knew that tears lay beneath her anxiety for the old lady, and upon an impulse—a surprising impulse for so taciturn a man—he said: 'Don't worry, Nurse—I've a feeling this good soul is going to be all right . . .'

Hope felt her heart tremble. She looked up swiftly, her eyes uttering mute thanks. She could not speak. Already she had uttered silent prayers for dear old Mrs. Tompkins and now, with a swift rush of faith, she knew that what Phillip Trent promised would be true.

'Patient is ready, sir . . .' said the anaesthetist, and with quiet composure Phillip set to work. Now all was forgotten but the importance of the job in hand—the slow, careful exploration . . . the checking and verification . . . the constant watch upon heart and pulse rate . . . the swift command from the surgeon—the prompt answer from Sister Theatre, extending the instruments . . . the thud of drum lids as each was plunged back into the sterilizer . . . the clink as they were laid ready upon the tray again . . . and all the time silence like a warm blanket in the tense room . . . the interest and apprehension, the anxiety and hope . . . and the minutes ticking by, marked only by the labored breathing of a brave, hard-working woman.

Remotely, in a detached part of her mind, Hope thought: *I should never have gone in for nursing—not theatre nursing! It eats at my heart too much . . . I feel too much, fear too much . . . Half an hour gone already, and more, much more, to be done . . .*

Mesmerized, she watched the surgeon's skilful hands. They were the hands of an artist, wielding his tools as if they were brushes preserving beauty for posterity. Sensitive, delicate in touch, precise and exquisitely careful. And fearless, too, as they plunged and explored and remedied. Above his mask his eyes were intent and serious—impossible to think that they had ever held any emotion!

Cold, methodical, scientifically accurate—was that his mind? Was there nothing more to it than that? Had they ever looked with tender concern upon the tired face which now, upon the operating table, looked so still and remote and pale? The wrinkled brow was at peace; the weary eyes slept. *God make her well again!* prayed Hope in a silent corner of her heart. *Give this man your power to heal . . . this man that I love . . .*

Because it was true, of course, deny it, fight it as she may. She had fallen in love with Phillip Trent as he stooped above Mrs. Tompkins in her bed down in Luke's ward, and she loved him now as he fought for the old lady's life. It did not matter that his eyes were cold and relentless right at this moment—the eyes of a stranger who awed and, at the same time, commanded respect. This was the man at work—the brilliant man who had saved lives before and would save them again . . .

And it did not matter if he never saw her, Staff Nurse Connell of Luke's ward, as anything but a figure in a starched uniform. All that did matter was that she would be allowed to see him occasionally, to help him, to serve him.

It was at that precise moment that her prayers were answered. There was a sudden lessening of tension in the room, a rising hope. She saw Phillip's eyes, alight with gratification, glance swiftly across at the assistant surgeon. His voice, charged with relief, said briefly: 'It's all right . . . we've got it in time . . . another six months, and it would have been too late . . .' And Hope felt a sob of sheer joy rise to her throat and hover there.

Phillip heard it, too. Whether anyone else

did, he had no idea, for the sound was merely a breathless whisper in the humid room. But he knew from where it came—from the heart which lay beneath Hope's amber-colored eyes; warm and vulnerable and tender, infinitely compassionate.

For a fleeting second his own eyes met hers—for a second only, during which his assistant surgeon dexterously swabbed the wound and stepped aside, but that second was long enough for a swift bond of understanding to leap between them. It was like an invisible cord uniting them.

When the operation was over and the frail, sleeping figure was borne away to comfort and rest, Phillip Trent astonished the entire theatre staff by turning to Nurse Connell and saying: 'Will you untie me, Nurse?' and without waiting for her answer walked off to the scrubbing-up room beyond. Sister Theatre raised surprised eyebrows, but dismissed the request with a shrug. The man was a newcomer and therefore ignorant of identities, but he should have been able to recognize a junior nurse—whose job it was to divest him of his surgical apron and gloves. She needed Staff Nurse Connell herself.

Inside the scrubbing-up room, Phillip shed his rubber boots and gloves. With trembling fingers Hope untied his apron and mask. Peeling off his tight-fitting cap he turned and faced her. 'You shouldn't take it so much to heart,' he said gently, his eyes cold no longer.

He moved toward a wash-basin and began to clean up. Hope removed her own mask, aware that her hands still trembled, and was bitterly ashamed of their betrayal, but relief made her weak and vulnerable. She had cared too deeply about old Mrs. Tompkins, and the fact that the old lady was now out of all danger awakened an extraordinary reaction. She wanted to cry.

She pushed back her hair with a limp, damp hand. 'I haven't been on theatre duty for some time,' she said weakly, ashamed because she found it necessary to excuse herself. Hesitantly, she raised her eyes and met his. He was drying his hands, regarding her intently as he did so. And his eyes were gentle and compassionate and understanding. He might never have been the cold, relentless man of the past hour.

He said briskly: 'She wasn't half so bad as I expected her to be. Most of the trouble was an obstruction—nothing more. I'm glad we operated, though, because it gave me a chance to check up on anything worse, and to prevent future complications. Old Mrs. Tompkins will be all right, Nurse. She's as strong as a horse, really, for all her fragility. These old women often are!'

His voice was light and reassuring—purposely, no doubt. He saw her distress and sought to comfort her, which revealed a humane side which few would ever suspect. She was so grateful to him that she could not speak. She merely nodded her head in mute acknowledgment, and he smiled suddenly—smiled more spontaneously and naturally than was his custom. It was a smile Felicity Drake would have given anything to receive.

'If I were you, Nurse Connell, I'd ask Sister's permission to go down to the kitchen and make a cup of tea.'

Laughter choked upon the lump in Hope's throat.

'I'm a nurse, sir! I have my job to do!'

He laughed with her, still regarding her with that strange intentness, still aware of the mutual attraction between them. Or was it only on his side? he wondered. Was it merely a figment of his own imagination? Perhaps. And yet, when first sensed, it seemed to flow like a strong, compelling current, carrying him upon the tide of its strength. He had never experienced anything like it before, and could not recognize its meaning, or its source, even now. All he knew was that he wanted to see more of this girl, to talk to her, to know her.

The swing door throbbed upon its hinges and Sister Theatre's voice called peremptorily: 'Have you finished with Staff Nurse, sir? I need her to attend to the instruments . . .'

The moment was shattered; their feeling of intimacy and understanding instantly dispelled. Hope pulled herself together and answered: 'Coming, Sister!' and, gathering up the discarded surgical gowns, carried them out to the hissing sterilizer. The door swung behind her, creaking upon its hinges. When Phillip emerged from the scrubbing-up room and left the theatre, all he saw was the back of her starched little back, hard at work.

CHAPTER EIGHT

St. Bede's Hospital had four main wards—Matthew, Mark, Luke, and John. Each had its own medical and surgical side, and a number of private rooms attached to it. The maternity wing was housed elsewhere in the town, and known as St. Mary's. The children's block was situated across the main courtyard, next door to the nurses' home. It was when he was crossing this courtyard, on his way from the children's wing to the main hospital building, that Michael Shearing came face to face with Charity Connell.

He stood for a moment, watching her approach. Her hand clasped the leash of a handsome labrador and, together, they moved in perfect unison. It was plain that the animal guarded his mistress most carefully and that she, in her turn, had implicit trust in him. She stepped out fearlessly and quite unselfconsciously. Nevertheless, when Michael stood still, watching her, she stood still also. For a brief imperceptible moment she waited, then said quietly: 'Who is it?'

He should have realized, of course, that her keenly attuned senses would warn her when someone approached, and when they paused abruptly. Yet it was some deeper instinct which told her that the footsteps had ceased because their owner was looking at her, studying her, waiting for her.

He felt as if he had been caught in some mischief and with a rueful laugh he answered: 'Sorry. It is I—Shearing.'

She experienced a strange little leap of her heart, and could not account for it. They had not met since their conversation in her treatment room a week ago. During that time she had heard various opinions of the new house physician—mostly from the nurses at meal times. He was rude, ill-mannered, opinionated. He was unsociable and, apparently, quite unsusceptible. He was darkly handsome and provocative, a challenge to any girl's femininity. To all these versions Charity listened, a smile hovering upon her soft lips, her thoughts secret. She alone, out of all the hospital, felt it within her power to glimpse the real Mike Shearing. She felt that already she had done so—briefly, disturbingly, unforgettably.

He had impressed himself upon her mind to a surprising degree. Accustomed as she was to forming her judgments of people entirely by their voices—which, after all, could reveal so much more than a face—she was disturbed by her impressions of this young doctor. That he was embittered out of all proportion to his years and experience was obvious; harder to discover was the reason for such bitterness. His voice was strong and virile and healthy, so he himself was all those things. But he was afraid of betraying himself—all the time he was afraid of betraying himself. He put up defenses against the world and defied anyone to break them down.

She smiled and said: 'Good afternoon, Doctor.'

He returned her greeting, and would have passed by, except that some unbidden instinct prompted him to wait.

'Where are you off to?' he asked.

'To the children's wards.' She smiled with pleasurable anticipation. 'I have my own treatment room over there, a replica of the main one.' He could tell from her tone that she enjoyed her time with the children. Her soft lips curved sweetly when she spoke of them.

She asked: 'How are you getting on, Doctor? Are you quite settled now?' She hardly knew why she asked, except that for some reason it was important to know. She was anxious about him. Right from the first she had been anxious about him. A man so guarded against hurt laid himself wide open to it.

He answered casually: 'More or less.' His tone implied indifference, but the truth was, she knew, that he cared acutely. The defensive, sensitive kind always did—and always denied it.

To ease the moment, Charity said easily: 'Residents' quarters are usually rather grim, aren't they? I hope you have a nice room.'

'Adequate,' he admitted.

There seemed nothing else to say, yet still they lingered. He said abruptly: 'How's Miss Ransom's leg coming along?' Not because it was really necessary for him to ask—he had examined it only this morning and found it considerably improved—but because it was good reason to detain her and because he hoped she would confirm his opinion that Miss Caroline Ransom would soon be able to go home.

'It is coming along splendidly, Doctor. It reaped dividends from the extra treatment. I should think another two should complete the cure. After that, if the trouble recurs, she can visit the hospital as an out-patient.'

'You think, then, that she could be discharged?'

'That is for you to say, Doctor—'

'I have my opinion. I'm asking for yours.' His voice was blunt, but his tone somehow conveyed a smile. She listened to it and liked it.

'Yes, I think she could be discharged. She is walking with the aid of a stick and managing quite well. It would not hurt her—it might even do her good, don't you think?—to be brought to the hospital from her home.'

'I'm glad we agree,' he said, and was wondering just what next he could say to detain her, when a voice brought him round in surprise. 'Ah, there you are, Doctor,' it said, and he saw Matron's regal figure emerging from the children's block and coming toward him. 'I'm glad we've met. It saves ringing you . . .'

'Ringing me, Matron?' he echoed politely.

'I was wondering whether you are free on Sunday—it is your off-duty day, I know, because I've checked on it and, if so, whether you would care to come along for a cocktail at six-thirty? It is just a little monthly gathering of mine.' She slipped her hand through Charity's arm as she spoke, adding: 'It includes my girls, of course. No party would be complete without them. Tell Faith and Hope, will you, Charity?'

'Of course I will,' Charity smiled, 'and you know our answer. We love your parties . . .' And away she went to the children's wards, the labrador padding gently beside her.

'Well, Doctor, will you come?'

He didn't want to. He wasn't a party man, and standing around with a glass in his hand, making polite conversation, was anathema to him. He was surprised when he heard himself saying: 'Thank you, Matron. I'd like to very much.' It was hypocrisy and he knew it, but, after all, the invitation was in the nature of a royal command—a junior doctor could not decline an invitation from the hospital's queen bee. Besides, the words were spoken and he could not retract. He did not wish to retract.

'Splendid,' said Matron.

Entering Matron's charming sitting-room the following Sunday evening, his eyes automatically searched for the blind girl. He experienced a swift disappointment because there was no sign of her. Neither she nor her sisters had yet arrived. He installed himself in a distant corner. Perhaps it was merely chance which arranged that he should have a direct view of the door, and of everyone who came through it, from that particular spot.

Doctor Willstack moved across and joined him. They had met only briefly since Michael's visit to the laboratory, and with his easy good nature Charles launched into conversation with him. The easiest way to draw out this silent young physician, he discovered, was to talk 'shop,' and in no time at all he realized that the doctor had something on his mind. It was when Matthew's ward was mentioned that Michael hesitated, as if wanting to discuss something—or someone? with a completely independent and detached person. Charles waited, as he had waited during Michael's laboratory visit, when he had sensed exactly the same thing.

But young Doctor Shearing lapsed into silence.

The room was becoming hazy with cigarette smoke, humming with conversation. Stephen Barlow, thought Charles Willstack shrewdly, would drink too much before the evening was out. Nearby, Stacey was discussing an article in the *Lancet* with Blake, the casualty officer. Matron was laughing heartily at some joke told by John Benham, the hospital secretary. He was a good-looking man, Charles thought, in his quiet undistinguished way. But he forgot all about the hospital secretary and young Doctor Shearing and everyone else when the door opened and Faith, Hope and Charity appeared.

Faith came first, her hand carelessly linked in Charity's, drawing her into the room, and through the gathering throng toward Matron. The woman's face lit up with deep affection when she saw them. 'Here come my children,' she said, and held out her motherly cheek for their greeting. Hope said; 'Sorry we're late, darling—Faith took so long in the bathroom we had to queue up at the door!'

'Libel!' cried Faith, and her lips parted in that rare and lovely smile. Doctor Willstack's heart skipped a beat. She had not seen him yet and, as yet, he did not wish her to. He knew what would happen when she did—she would retire into her shell, leaving him out in the cold. He wanted to look upon her real and natural self for a little longer, for he had secretly known that outside the laboratory she would be like this—warm and charming and at ease. So far, he had been unable to get her to discuss anything but work.

John Benham, in his fatherly fashion, brought cocktails for the girls. He seemed to play host here very naturally, thought Charles, and his perceptive grey eyes flickered from the hospital secretary's kindly face to Matron's motherly one. They were about the same age, both unmarried. A middle-aged romance? he thought fleetingly. Well, why not? Middle-aged romances were very often successful, sometimes the best . . .

He dismissed the thought, turning his attention back to Faith. She wore a simple grey dress, with what he believed was called a 'boat-shaped' neck-line and a ballet skirt. Soft, filmy stuff—chiffon, was it, or georgette? As a bachelor he was somewhat ignorant about women's fashions, but whatever it was, the material suited Faith. It clung to her slender figure in all the places it should cling, he thought appreciatively. Her hair, smooth and glossy and coiled on the nape of her neck like a ballerina's, shone like a raven's wing tonight. She was lovely, but cold. Cold only on the surface, he thought. Beneath lay a sleeping fire.

He was able to watch her unnoticed for a few more minutes before she turned and saw him. Her eyes reflected a brief surprise—and something more. But what? He could not tell, for up went the barriers of her reserve again and away went her smile. She greeted him formally, and he said: 'Can't you forget for once that I'm your boss? Why not pretend that we're a man and a woman, for a change?'

It was fortunate that conversation now eddied about them like the hum of an energetic hive. They were as isolated as on a desert island, able to talk with equal privacy. He took hold of her wrist and drew her through the crush. A window seat flanked a small bay window, and he pressed her down on it, gently and firmly. 'Drink up,' he said, 'and relax. We're not in the lab, now, you know.' Obediently, she lifted her glass to her lips, hoping he did not observe the trembling of her hand, wondering why she should be so shaken by this meeting. She had expected him to be there, for these monthly gatherings of Matron's always included the medical staff. What she had not expected was his greeting, his immediate possession of her, and—most disconcerting of all—his form of attack. *Why not pretend that we're a man and woman . . . ?*

Pretend! A man like this would not let you forget!

He took her empty glass and brought her another. 'Don't go away,' he commanded, 'I want to talk to you . . .' If she had wanted to go away, she couldn't have managed it, for now the little sitting-room was filled to overflowing; people pressed close. The last arrivals entered —Phillip Trent, with a tall, grey-haired woman slightly older than himself, and bearing a strong resemblance. A sister?

Charles was back, saying: 'Here you are—a couple of these ought to chip the icicles off you!'

A smile flickered across her mouth and he continued hopefully: 'That's better. I'll ply you with these until you thaw, Miss Connell. I've been waiting for that ever since we met.'

'I don't know what you mean.'

'Oh yes, you do! You're too intelligent a person to sidestep the truth in that fashion. You don't like me, do you?'

'I don't know you, Doctor Willstack.'

'Charles is the name—outside the lab, and in, for all I care.'

'That is the trouble,' she heard herself saying. 'You don't care about informality in the laboratory.'

He moved impatiently.

'Of course I don't—so long as the work is done, and done well. What do you expect me to do—crack a whip?'

'Of course not. But we are unaccustomed to easy *camaraderie* up there.'

He was not the type to criticize his predecessor. All he said was: 'You'll get used to it, Faith. And like it, I hope. Don't expect me to change. I'm not the sort of man who can. Whether I call the lab. boy Tommy or Watkins, the orders I give him are still orders. Whether I use your Christian name—which I much prefer to Miss Connell—or not, you're still assistant pathologist and I the chief. That doesn't mean that I expect you to bend the knee to me. I merely expect you to work well, and that comes easily to you because you're keen on your job. Pathology interests you. That goes for me, too, so by all the laws of logic we ought to get along nicely together, you and I. Inside the laboratory—and out.'

She didn't know what to say. His words made sense, but still she found it hard to achieve an easy social footing with him. He sensed her thoughts and smiled with understanding. This girl had been refrigerated in old Doctor Walker's cold régime; she couldn't be expected to melt overnight. He said gently: 'Let's change the subject, shall we? Tell me what sort of social life this hospital has to offer.'

She smiled at him gratefully—and more easily than hitherto. 'Well,' she said, warming to the subject, 'the highlight of the year is the Hospital Ball. Then we really go to town! The nurses save up for new evening gowns for fifty-two weeks out of fifty-two—and consider it worth it. It's held in the County Hall—red carpet, awnings, banked-up flowers, everything! Cinderella's ball come to life—and all the Cinderellas of the hospital shedding their uniforms and blossoming overnight. The staff are invited by rota, of course, because naturally some have to be on duty—' She broke off, embarrassed by her unusual flow of words. She had not realized how easy it would be to talk to this man. His exuberant personality had almost overcome her right from the beginning—and coupled with this was the constant memory of their first encounter. That appalling, unfortunate encounter! She flushed at the recollection of it. What a fool she had made of herself, mistaking him for an orderly and bossing him around!

He saw her flush and said gently: 'Go on—I'm interested.'

'But you must know what a Hospital Ball is like! You've held a hospital appointment before.'

He said seriously: 'I've been working too hard, Faith, to play. I've taken all my exams since the war —I was caught up in that during my first medical year, and it put a brake on my progress for some time. I had a great deal to catch up when I came out. So, you see, I've had to devote all my time to study, even when I got my first job. Even more, then, because my aim was to get a chief pathologist's appointment and that meant working round the clock very often.'

She regarded him with fresh interest. Had she misjudged this man? It seemed so. He gave the impression of being too light-hearted for serious study, but what he said was undoubtedly true. Work, and hard work, got a man to the position he now held.

But she still considered he should take life more seriously. Guessing her thought, he said with a smile: 'Life is real and life is earnest to you, isn't it, Faith?'

Her lovely eyes met his.

'Shouldn't it be?' she asked innocently.

He was so touched he could not speak. Momentarily, his hand covered hers. He wanted to awaken her, to touch the secret places of her heart, to stir up that sleeping fire at the core of her—and yet she was so lovely as she was. Like a Madonna, he thought gently, and answered: 'Providing we don't forget how to laugh, yes. We can be serious beneath our gaiety, Faith. And some day I'll prove it to you.'

She was stirred by the touch of his hand, and alarmed by the reaction. Afraid, too, lest he should sense it. She need not have feared, for he withdrew, saying lightly: 'Will you grant me a favor?'

'What is it?' she asked in surprise.

'Give me the pleasure of your company at the ball. We'll both be free—the laboratory closes at night! Will you take a male Cinderella to his first hospital dance—

Princess Charming?'

She threw back her lovely head and laughed. He was irresistible. 'How can I refuse?' she asked.

'You might have been booked up—'

'No. We always go in a party—my sisters and I; Matron and John Benham; Stephen Barlow and others. We'd be glad for you to join us.'

'That isn't exactly what I want, but it will do to go on. I accept, providing,' he finished with a twinkle, 'I'm your official escort—partners, for that night at least, outside the laboratory, as well as in . . .'

CHAPTER NINE

Charity was wearing chartreuse green, against which her pale gold hair was reflected like a daffodil. She wore it loose, to her shoulders, the tips faintly curled, and she had brushed it until it gleamed. When she stooped it fell like a curtain across one cheek. Michael watched the gentle swing of it—smooth and glossy and silken—as she bent to stroke Matron's fabulous persian cat. Her sensitive fingers groped toward the hearth-rug, found the rich, warm coat, and caressed it. She knew she was sitting beside the fire because she could feel the heat of it upon her right cheek, and she knew that Confucius was curled upon the hearth-rug at her feet. She could hear his rich purr, close beside her.

Michael said: 'So Mustard, poor fellow, has to stay at home tonight?'

It was the first chance he had had to speak to her. From her moment of entry he had waited for the opportunity—perhaps because he found her easy to talk to, or perhaps because he was shy of everyone else. Whatever the reason, Charity Connell was, apart from his hostess and Doctor Willstack (who had forgotten him the moment Faith Connell appeared), the only person in the room who was not chilled by his bitter silence.

If she could see me, he wondered, would she be chilled, too? Michael knew that people did not take to him easily. As far as he was concerned, that did not matter. All he wanted was work, anyway. As a small boy he had been friendly, affectionate, full of life, but he had put all that nonsense behind him. He could get along well enough without people, without friends . . .

All the same—he did want to talk to Charity Connell.

She looked up with a smile, her beautiful sightless eyes lighting up with pleasure. He silenced the inner compassion of his heart, for he scorned sentiment. All the same, it seemed tragic that eyes bereft of light could convey so much radiance.

She said: 'Hello, Doctor Shearing. Yes, Mustard has to stay at home on these occasions. Actually, he enjoys it—Home Sister spoils him to death. So do the domestic staff. I expect when I get back he'll be asleep through overeating!'

He laughed with her. He was surprised how easy it was to laugh.

'He's a magnificent animal. How long have you had him?'

'Four years. I had to go on a waiting list, you see. More and more dogs are being trained for the blind these days.'

'And a good thing, too. Where did you get him?'

'From a Guide Dog School in Exeter. When my turn came, I had to go there and stay at the school for a month, to work with him and to get to know him. And for him to get to know me, too!' She smiled. 'Oh yes, I had to learn, as well as Mustard! We manage each other, you know.'

'I always thought guide dogs are Alsatians.'

'A good many are, but they are reserved for the men.'

She stretched out her left hand, felt the empty seat beside her, and patted it. 'Do sit down,' she said. 'I'll get a crick in my neck if I keep on looking up at you!' When he was seated, she said: 'That sounds silly, I suppose, but I do look at people, you know. I have my own picture of them. Sometimes my sisters and I play a game which I enjoy very much. I tell them my idea of what a person looks like, and they give me points for accuracy! It's fun.'

'And the average?' he asked.

'About seven out of ten. I'm proud of that! I fall down on details, of course: shapes of noses, and features which I can't estimate without touch, but height, build, type, and so on, I can guess pretty well. Voices tell so much more than people who have their sight realize.'

'And mine?' he asked curiously. 'Does mine tell you anything?'

'Of course! It tells me a lot.'

'I wonder if I ought to ask what?'

'There's a challenge in that!' She laughed. 'I'll take it up!' She settled herself comfortably, Confucius curled handsomely upon her lap. 'I had a drink somewhere—' Her sensitive fingers reached toward the mantelpiece, where she had placed her glass before picking up the cat. Michael forestalled her and put the glass in her hand.

'Cigarette?' he asked, and gave her one, placing a light to its tip. She smoked quite naturally, and more gracefully than most women, the delicacy of her hands lending beauty to the movements.

'Go on—' he said, aware of an excited curiosity.

She smiled, leaned her head against the upholstered settee back, and said: 'You are dark and rugged and angry.'

'Angry!' He laughed shortly, finding himself shocked at the description.

'Your voice is angry,' she said gently. 'But inside, you are not that sort of a person at all. You are strong physically, but not emotionally—not strong, that is, in the way you think.'

He asked abruptly: 'And in what way *do* I think myself strong? Can you tell me that?'

She did not miss the truculent note in his voice.

'In self-reliance. You believe you have no need of people, that you can get along well enough without them, but you are wrong.'

'*You* are wrong! Of course I need people. What doctor doesn't?'

'I did not mean as patients—and you know it. Don't sidestep. You asked for my opinion of you—'

'I asked what you saw, what my voice told you—'

'And you do not like my answer.' She shook her head at him gently. 'Do any of us like the truth, I wonder? I expect I should hate it if anyone handed it to me.'

He was silent. He looked down at his hands, unable to meet the disconcerting gaze of those sightless eyes. Then he said quietly: 'The truth about you would not hurt. You are gentle and courageous. You are afraid of nothing. I envy you.'

To his surprise her hand came out and

covered his. She knew instinctively where it lay and the movement was as natural as breathing. 'We are all afraid of something,' she said. 'I have my fears, too. Fears of the future. Of being alone. Fears of losing Mustard. Fears of losing my way—not merely physically, but in life. More than all, fears of dependence and helplessness . . .'

His fingers closed over hers protectively. He held them tightly, briefly, and then released them, but not before she felt their betraying tremble.

She forced lightness into her voice. 'This is a party, Doctor! Let's enjoy it, shall we?'

But after what she had said, he could not. Was he an angry person? Was he suspicious, resentful, steeling himself against the world and everyone in it? Her words implied so. Abruptly, he asked: 'Please go on. I'm sorry I took your description so badly. It shocked me.'

'You need not heed it. I may be wrong.'

'You are not wrong. I do shun people. I don't *want* to need others!'

'But we all need them! You, as much as I and the next person. We can none of us live in an isolated world, Doctor, self-imposed or otherwise. Has it never occurred to you that other people need *you*?'

'Medically, perhaps. In no other way.'

'What about personal relationships? Family life? Love?'

'Sentiment!' he scoffed. 'I've no time for

sentiment.'

She regarded him with undisguised pity. 'Then I'm sorry for you, Doctor Shearing,' she said and, shooing the cat off her lap, rose to leave him. She could hear Hope's voice a little way off, directly ahead. She had only to take a few steps forward to reach her side, and there was no other voice barring the way. But Michael Shearing, against his will, reached out and caught her wrist.

'Don't go, Charity!'

His use of her name—so naturally, so easily—surprised him. But it did not surprise her. Already, in her mind, she thought of him as Michael. She said sternly: 'I certainly shall if you intend to talk nonsense! No time for sentiment, indeed! Life is based upon sentiment, whatever the cynics might declare! And you are not a cynic—not really, no matter how hard you try. The most callous doctor must feel a pang of sentiment at times, that I firmly believe. About his work, his hospital, his patients—his wife, his children, his mother!'

She sensed his withdrawal as she said the word 'mother,' and something inside her made her pause. Beyond the screen of her eyes she sensed his tightened mouth, his flared nostrils, his darkening brow. What unhappy spot had she unwittingly touched; what vulnerable wound had she probed? She said gently: 'I'm sorry, Michael, if I said the wrong thing. Forget my silly impressions—how can I be expected to see the truth? I play a child's game, nothing more . . .' Her voice faltered and died.

'Not a child's game,' he said softly. 'An adult one, and an unerring one . . .' He felt humbled by her perception, and suddenly he wanted to talk to her—intimately, personally, in some quiet place where no intruders could enter, where no other voices trespassed. It was impossible here—in the midst of laughter and gossip and a milling crowd. He wanted to take her by the hand and steal away —but where? He wanted to confide in her, to seek her assurance, to draw upon her integrity and strength, to warm himself with her comfort. He wanted to keep her close beside him; to protect and cherish her. The desire for these things was so strong that he stood silent and afraid. Betrayal, he knew, could come so easily . . .

She said: 'I hear Hope's voice—she is calling me—'

The moment was over. He knew with complete certainty that he would have no further opportunity to get her alone this evening. She gave him her lovely smile and crossed to Hope, who was saying: 'Charity—come here and be introduced! This is Mr. Trent's sister—'

Agatha Trent was in her forties—a few years her brother's senior. She was tall, well built, and what was called in her girlhood 'bonny.' By today's standards she was just plain fat. She was also remarkably like her brother, but whereas the Trent features were handsome in a man, they were far from handsome in a woman, which was a pity, thought Hope, who liked Agatha at once.

Standing behind Charity Connell, Agatha observed the silent figure of Michael Shearing, and her good-natured face broke into a smile. 'Mike!' she cried, still holding the blind girl's slim fingers in her welcoming hand. 'How good to see you!'

And it was. She knew, of course, that Michael had got the house physician's appointment at St. Bede's, but since then she had heard nothing of him. His path had not crossed Phillip's again. No doubt they would hear all about it from Colonel Shearing, she had thought, in due course; until then, she was not bothering to make inquiries, despite the maternal anxiety she had always felt for his son. Michael was a reserved young man, and long ago Agatha had realized that if she wanted to retain his confidence she had to respect that reserve. She was his godmother, and had always taken her responsibilities toward him seriously.

Phillip's strong hand rested briefly upon his shoulder, welcoming him. They were good friends, lasting friends, Mike thought gratefully. With only two such friends in life, a man would do well. He suppressed the thought—the disturbing thought which leapt unbidden to his mind—that to be complete a man needed more than friendship. He needed love, sentiment, all the things he professed to scorn.

He heard Charity's voice, sincerely pitying, echoing in his mind, and resented it. Why *should* she feel sorry for him, just because he was self-reliant and unsentimental? These things made him strong! He had clung to them since the age of thirteen, and a pitiful, vulnerable thirteen he must have been, he realized now, to care so deeply . . .

He heard Phillip's voice saying: 'When are you coming to see us, Mike? When are you free? It seems a long time since you dropped in, and I don't mean since you joined St. Bede's. Long before that, exams robbed us of you. Now you're free of them, for the time being, I hope you're going to make it up to us?'

'Of course he is,' said Agatha firmly. 'He's coming to see us on his very next off duty, aren't you, Mike? I'll ring your father and get him to come along, too.'

'If you succeed,' grinned Mike, 'you'll achieve a miracle. You know Dad hates leaving his house slippers and his pipe.'

'Then he can bring them with him,' said Agatha blandly, 'and you,' she finished, 'can bring these girls. It's a long time since I had the chance to entertain young people, so don't refuse, Miss Connell!'

Had I really opened my mouth to do so? Hope wondered. She wanted to refuse, and could not.

Charity said: 'How lovely! Thank you very much, Miss Trent. We'd love to come. Faith, too? There are three of us, you know, and we do everything together.'

'Of course, Faith, too. I've heard so much about the St. Bede's triplets from Matron that I shall look forward to getting to know them. Isn't that Faith, sitting over there by the window, talking to the good-looking fair man?'

'Yes,' said Hope.

'She's lovely, isn't she?' Charity said enthusiastically. 'Her voice is like music and the feel of her hair is like silk, and she has the gentlest hands. Hope's voice is like sparkling wine and her laughter like sunshine. And I know they are both pretty.'

Agatha felt a lump in her throat, the prick of tears behind her eyes. Pretty! she thought! My dear child, I wish you could see yourself . . .

Aloud, she said: 'You are all remarkably alike—but I suppose it isn't so remarkable, really, in view of the relationship!' She had to force a light, practical note in her voice to steady it. 'Well,' she finished briskly, 'that is settled, then? When are you off duty next, Mike?'

'On Saturday, unless Doctor Stacey asks me

to take over.'

'I know Doctor Stacey,' Agatha said with determination, 'so he'll take his instructions from me before I leave tonight!'

'Talking of leaving,' put in Phillip, 'that applies to me—now.' He glanced at his watch and noted in some concern that it was seven forty-five. He was dining with Felicity at eight—not, as she had wanted, in her own exquisite little flat, but in the Marine Hotel Grill Room. He always shunned Felicity's intimate little dinner parties, although he couldn't think why.

Agatha said: 'You can't go yet, Phillip—you have to drive me home.'

'I'll take a taxi, and leave you the car.'

'Brothers!' Agatha rolled her eyes ceilingwards.

'I'll see you home, Agatha,' Michael offered, but she shook her maternal head.

'No need—I'm quite a good driver. Better than my brother, although he'd never admit it. Ask Hibbs.'

Phillip's stern face relaxed in a smile. 'We won't start *that* discussion,' he said. 'I must be off.'

His eyes alighted briefly upon Hope, revealing nothing, but observing much. Quite suddenly he didn't want to go.

Agatha Trent was saying to Charity: 'I know you well by sight, my dear. I've seen you round the town with a very handsome dog.'

'Mustard. Isn't he beautiful?'

'His coat is the color of sherry—golden-brown,' Hope put in. 'He's no right to have hair that color —it rivals my own!' Everyone laughed.

Agatha said firmly: 'Oh no, it doesn't, my dear—your hair is the color of autumn leaves in the park . . .'

She broke off abruptly, a shiver in her heart. The park! A sparkling lake . . . tables beneath gay umbrellas in summer, but standing like lost, forgotten people in winter . . .

Forgotten people with shabby feet kicking up the fallen leaves as they walked slowly by . . .

'We often walk in the park, Mustard and I,' said Charity. 'There's a little café by the lake where I stop and have tea. Do you know it, Miss Trent?'

'Yes. I know it. I've never been inside, but I passed that way today.'

CHAPTER TEN

Walking across the park, Charity could feel the breeze upon her face. It was sharp and invigorating, with an autumnal tang about it, whipping color into her cheeks. It carried the smell of wood smoke and burning leaves. She sniffed appreciatively. Somewhere in the park they were burning sweepings, but the gardeners' besoms had not yet reached the ground she trod. She was glad of that. She kicked her feet pleasurably among the fallen leaves, delighting in the sound. Even so, as children, had she walked with her sisters, hand in hand, she in the center, kicking up clouds of dry, rustling leaves and squealing her delight.

She heard the soft pad of Mustard's paws and the short scuffling sounds they made. Rustle, scuff . . . rustle, scuff . . . He was panting with pleasure, reveling in the clear afternoon. Soon, she thought, it would be winter, with no mounds of leaves in the gutters, no whispering carpet on which to tread. Just the cold air whistling through bare branches—sometimes sharp, sometimes kind; sometimes fierce and biting. Whatever the weather, she and Mustard would come for their daily walk, unless there were icy patches to catch the unwary. And whatever the season, there was always the tang of salt in the air, blown inland from the waterfront.

It was only a short walk from the park gates to the lake and the little café. She could always tell when she approached. First there would be the wide curving sweep of the main drive from the gates—Mustard kept well to the side here, especially as they rounded the bend, for sometimes delivery vans going to and from the café swept round unexpectedly; even the sound of their engines was obscured by the gigantic rhododendron bushes on either side. Once round the bend, the wide sweep of water lay ahead, lapping gently against the banks; sometimes turbulent, if the weather was rough.

Charity could imagine the scene vividly, for Hope, with her zest for life, had once described it to her, and Faith, with her quiet love of beauty, had added the rest. Between them they had painted the world with delicate precision for their blind sister, supplying details of color and form which she could only picture with her mind's eye. This she did not mind, for her senses of touch and hearing were doubly acute.

She was blessed with a skill denied ordinary human beings, who thought themselves equipped with all the senses and pitied her deficiency—the skill to hear undertones of beauty in everyday sounds, to feel planes and textures of things with sharp appreciation. What life had denied her on the one hand, it atoned for a hundredfold in other ways. I'm lucky, she told herself, and meant it. I'm luckier than most people in the world.

Today she felt exhilarated. Life tingled in her veins like wine. She was young and healthy and the world was a golden bowl enclosing her in enchantment. Beside the lake she broke into a gentle run, Mustard trotting beside her. Children were playing nearby—she could hear their laughter and the sound of a thudding ball. It fell close beside her. She felt the rush of air as it whizzed by.

'Look *out*, silly! That lady's blind!'

The child's voice echoed clearly upon the breeze. So did the answering one.

'It's *you* that's silly! She's *not* blind—she's only exercising her dog!'

Oh, bless you, *bless you*! Charity thought. That was the sort of compliment she liked to receive. Laughing, she turned and waved her hand in their direction, hoping—believing—that the children waved back. She was right. 'Hello!' they cried. 'What's his name?'

She called back: 'Mustard!' and heard the swift rush of their feet. The next minute they were fondling him, fussing over him. 'What a funny name for a dog!' one cried. 'I like it,' declared the other. 'I suppose you call him that because he has a golden sort of coat?'

'Among other reasons.' Charity smiled, and wondered briefly why a sudden silence fell. Then she knew. The sudden contact of a sturdy young body told her she was facing slightly out of focus. She turned fully in their direction.

'I *told* you she was—' The child's voice broke off, embarrassed and shy.

Charity laughed. 'Well, I had you fooled for a while, didn't I?'

Sharp with relief, the children's voices echoed her laughter.

'You know,' said the second child, 'no one would ever know you were blind! You don't *look* blind.'

'I'm glad.'

'Is it awful?' asked the first curiously. Apparently the second, perhaps older and more sensitive, nudged him vigorously, for he subsided abruptly with a jerking movement which made Charity smile.

'Just a nuisance sometimes,' she told them frankly. 'In other ways it's rather nice. I don't have to see the things I don't want to see—ugly things, for instance. I can have my own pictures instead.'

'It seems a pity,' said the older child, 'that you can't see Mustard.'

'Oh, but I can! I know his shape so well, and the lines of his face—it's a very handsome face, isn't it?—and the color of his coat, and the lovely smoothness of it. I can see him just as well as you can, really.'

'Gosh!'

A woman's voice, a short distance away, called authoritatively.

'Bother—we've got to go! Will you be coming to the park again?'

'Almost every day.'

'May we play with Mustard sometime?'

'Providing you don't tire him out, or take him far away.'

'We won't—honest we won't! We'll just play with him around here, in this wide space.'

'All right. There's your mother calling you again. You'd better go.'

United splutters answered her.

'*She's* not our mother! She's only Mabel, who takes us out.' A profound sigh followed. 'And she only wants to go now because she'll see George on his beat if we do. He passes the main gates at four o'clock. She's moony about him.'

'He's moony about her, too. Aren't grown-ups silly?'

'Awfully!' Charity agreed solemnly, and listened with a smile to their reluctant departure.

She felt Mustard straining toward the right and knew what that meant. Tea for herself, and for him; brief freedom from the leash. Once Faith had described the little café as a Japanese pagoda, and, to give her an idea of its architectural lines, modeled it in miniature from cardboard. Charity's sensitive fingers had picked out every curving line of the roof, every door and window, every step. There were four leading to the entrance. Mustard padded up them, paused while she opened the door, and accompanied her inside. He knew her customary table—the second on the right, beside the window.

It was a small room, with wooden walls and floor. At the end was a counter, with glass-topped dishes containing sandwiches and packets of biscuits, shelves with lemonade and ginger beer bottles, an urn for tea or coffee. But the woman who ran the place never made

Charity's tea from the urn. She brought her a small pot, containing exactly two cups, and she placed it upon a tray in exactly the same position each time, watching over her like a mother while her unerring fingers poured. She could never quite believe in Charity's amazing independence. One day, she felt sure, the girl would pour the tea into the saucer or, at least, let it overflow. But she never did. One tip of the cream jug—and always at the same unerring angle—was sufficient for the milk; the same angle for the teapot, but held a little longer. With the fingers of her left hand, Charity checked the placing of the cup, and from the sound of the running liquid seemed able to tell just when enough had been poured.

Nevertheless, the woman hovered. She was middle-aged, faded, rather shabby, but all Charity knew was that her voice was gentle and musical. There was refinement and culture in its tones. Charity wondered how a woman of obvious breeding came to be doing such a job, but widowhood apparently made it necessary. 'And I've never been trained for any sort of a career,' she told her. Whatever the reasons, Charity was glad she was there. She liked her and enjoyed talking to her.

Sometimes she made Charity laugh, describing the odd assortment of people who dropped in. For the most part it was children for lemonades and cake, but there were 'regulars,' too. Charity was one. There was also an eccentric old artist who had been painting the lake for years and never painted anything else; a few nursemaids; one or two solitary old ladies who exercised their dogs in the park and a few retired old gentlemen who exercised themselves. Winter, of course, was quieter than summer. In summer she had extra help, but in the winter she ran the place single-handed. Today marked the end of her summer 'relief'—so for this afternoon, at least, she had time to stand and talk to Charity.

'That faithful animal of yours is having a wonderful time rolling over and over in the leaves,' she observed with a laugh. 'He really is a beautiful creature. His coat blends magnificently with the autumn colors.' She broke off abruptly, then finished: 'There is a woman making a fuss over him now. Does everyone?'

'Almost everyone. I hope it won't spoil him!' Charity sounded like a proud and anxious mother, and the woman regarded her with a gentle smile.

'He is too devoted to his mistress for there to be any danger of that,' she said reassuringly. Charity had a feeling that she was going to continue, but, instead, she fell suddenly silent. 'I must get along to the kitchen,' she said abruptly. 'Just ring this bell if there is anything more you want.' She left the bell close by Charity's hand and departed.

Charity sipped her tea, listening to the relief

woman's listless chanting in the kitchen, and the distant squeals of children at play, and the wild cry of seagulls flying inland. That meant rain, according to the old salts down on the waterfront. Then another sound cut into the moment—the sound of the main door opening and shutting and a woman's footsteps approaching. Heavy footsteps, but a woman's all the same, Charity judged.

She was right. A voice said amiably: 'I hoped it would be you, Miss Connell—I felt sure that was your dog outside.'

It was Agatha Trent; Charity recognized her voice at once and felt a swift surge of pleasure. She had liked Agatha from their first moment of meeting —her brother, too, although he had actually contributed little to the conversation. She flashed a welcoming smile and said: 'Miss Trent—how lovely!'

'May I join you?'

'Of course. I'll ring for more tea.'

Charity did so, and Agatha pulled out a chair beside her, saying: 'I'm glad we met—it saves my 'phoning about Saturday. You and your sisters are coming to see us, aren't you? I was going to ring Doctor Shearing with instructions to bring you—'

'There's no need to do that! We'll find our way.'

Charity had an idea Doctor Shearing might not like escorting three young women. She had a further idea that Doctor Shearing did not like young women—or any women, for that matter. She felt a swift pang of pity in her gentle heart—pity for a man who shunned sentiment and prided himself upon his supreme self-sufficiency.

'Shall we say seven?' Agatha asked. 'That will give us time for a cocktail before dinner.'

'That will be lovely.' Charity was aware that, although Miss Trent had her mind on the conversation, her attention was slightly distracted. 'Are you impatient for your tea?' she asked. 'I'll ring again . . .'

But at that moment the door from the kitchen opened and shuffling footsteps approached. It wasn't the nice proprietor, Charity realized in surprise, and heard a different voice say sulkily: 'Is it tea you want?'

Agatha said good-humoredly: 'If it isn't too much trouble!' Her warm voice quivered with suppressed laughter. Charity checked a smile and said: 'Is the proprietor busy?'

The woman answered insolently: 'Seems so, don't it, since she arst me to take your order. Anything to eat?'

'Just tea,' said Agatha firmly, and a voice from the main door said: 'That goes for me, too—' and there was Michael Shearing, his broad bulk filling the aperture. For Charity, his voice filled the room, making her most vividly aware of his vitality.

'Mike dear!' Agatha exclaimed. 'This is a surprise! Is everyone walking in the park today?'

'It seems so,' he laughed. 'I don't know what made me, I must admit. I had a free half-hour between duties and wanted a breath of air.' He had reached their table now. Charity felt his eyes upon her. 'May I?' he asked, his hand upon the back of a chair.

'By all means,' agreed Agatha. 'You're just in time to pay for our tea, Mike, and to confirm about Saturday. Will seven suit you?'

'Splendidly. Would you like me to bring the Misses Connell?'

Why was it, Charity wondered, that one sensed an underlying mockery, a sneer, almost a resentment in his voice?

'There's no need—' she began, but Agatha spoke at the same time, obscuring her words. 'That's just what I was suggesting,' she said. 'Ah, good—here comes the tea.'

The same slatternly footsteps came and went. As Agatha poured for herself and Michael, the young man said: 'What a funny little place! I hope the tea makes up for the slattern who served it.'

'I've never known her to serve before,' said Charity, eager to defend the place where she spent so many happy hours. 'The proprietor is a charming woman.'

'Then it's a pity she wasn't here to serve us,' Michael answered. 'She might have remembered to supply teaspoons!'

'Don't be fussy,' Agatha chaffed good-naturedly. Michael, she felt, was in one of his 'dark moods' and should not be pandered to. 'You can't have everything in this life.'

'A teaspoon isn't everything,' he argued, 'merely something with which to cool one's tea.'

'Let's be vulgar and blow on it,' said Agatha jovially, and Charity laughed.

'I must go,' she said a minute or two later. 'I have to give Matron another treatment at five-thirty.'

Michael rose. 'Shall I call Mustard?' he asked, opening the door for her.

'Please. He'll come if you whistle.'

But Mustard was already there, sitting upon the doorstep, waiting for his mistress. She fondled his patient head. 'I know what he wants,' she said. 'The proprietor always spoils him with a saucerful of tea before we leave.'

'That's easily remedied,' said Michael. 'Come on, Mustard old boy!' And he poured tea into his saucer for the dog, who followed him obediently, pausing to lick the doctor's hand before drinking. Charity heard the ecstatic sound and said in surprise: 'He likes you!'

Michael said wryly: 'Is that so very surprising?'

'In a way,' Charity admitted with characteristic frankness, 'since you yourself don't like people.'

'But I do like dogs,' Michael retorted. 'They

are so much more faithful.'

'Don't be a cynic, Mike!' Agatha's friendly voice was almost sharp. 'I'll walk as far as the gates with you, Charity, and Michael here can settle the bill.'

Michael grinned. He would take any amount of bullying from Agatha Trent. 'A pleasure,' he assured them, and then, with a rare burst of sincerity, added: 'I came in with that intention, anyway. Mustard told me outside that his mistress was here, and I saw you walking ahead of me, Agatha, and surmised that you had joined her.'

He did not add that some instinct over which he had no control had compelled him to seek Charity in the park today, knowing it was her half-day. One admission, felt his proud heart, was enough.

He rang the bell, and a moment or two later the slattern appeared.

'That'll be four-'n'-six,' she droned, in a voice which told him plainly what a nuisance they all were.

Mustard was leading Charity down the steps outside at that moment. Agatha stood by the door, waiting. She said abruptly to the woman: 'Is the owner away this afternoon?'

The woman looked at her with bored indifference.

'Mrs. Shearing, y'mean? No—she's back there in the kitchen, doing my washing-up. Dunno why. Told me to take over out 'ere, which is summat I've never known 'er to do before. Can't think why, but she didn't seem to *want* to come out . . .'

CHAPTER ELEVEN

Walking down the steps, Michael said: 'Funny. I thought she said Shearing.'

'She did say Shearing, Michael.'

'She couldn't! The only Shearings in Highcliffe are Dad and myself. Look in the phone book.'

'Perhaps this woman isn't in the phone book.'

'It must have been Shearer,' Michael decided. 'There's a jeweler of that name in the High Street, and a dentist on Plymouth Road.'

But it wasn't Shearer, and he knew it. Agatha knew it, too. The slattern had spoken the name with the assurance born of familiarity. The woman behind the scenes was named Shearing and that was all there was to it. Agatha said with forced jocularity: 'You Shearings aren't that exclusive, Michael! Thousands of people up and down the country may have your name.'

'But not in Highcliffe,' Michael persisted.

'Perhaps it is a distant aunt you've never heard of,' Agatha said lightly.

'Dad has only one sister and she swopped

the name of Shearing for her husband's years ago. And she's out in Australia getting rich on wool.'

'So she isn't likely to be managing a little café in a public park in Devon! That proves the name is mere coincidence, nothing more.'

And so they dismissed it. At the main park gates Michael and Charity turned toward the hospital, Mustard padding contentedly between them. For a moment Agatha watched their departure, reflecting that she had only once before seen Michael so relaxed and at peace, and that was the other night at Matron's party when, as now, he had been talking to Charity Connell. The realization brought a stirring of happiness in Agatha's heart. A girl like Charity was just what Michael needed; a girl to awaken the dormant chivalry within him and to restore his shattered faith in women.

Feeling oddly content, Agatha allowed her mind to leap forward to Saturday. It wasn't so far off, and they would be together again, those two—the dark, unhappy young doctor and the fair, serene young woman. They would be together beneath her roof, and her match-making heart delighted in the thought.

And then, with a strange quickening of hope and fear, she thought of something else and someone else. It wasn't true, of course. It wasn't even possible. All the same—if it *were* . . .

Abruptly, and with characteristic impulsiveness, Agatha Trent turned and retraced her steps.

* * *

Phillip Trent and his sister lived in an old white house on the top of Beacon Hill. From its mellow windows could be seen the wide sweep of bay and the fine mesh of streets which hugged the waterfront like a cluttered shawl. It was a picturesque view of which Phillip never tired.

On a clear day the fishing boats of Highcliffe's ancient fleet looked like flies caught in the spider's web of the sea. Today had been such a day, with clear autumn sunshine sprinkling the waves with a million scattered sequins. Most of Highcliffe's fishing vessels carried the deep red sails of old, a warm and vivid contrast with the fathomless green of the waters. Now the afternoon was drawing to a close, sinking into the horizon like a blazing fire, until the whole bay was dyed in its glory.

Phillip stood at the window of his study, ostensibly admiring the view but in reality watching the wrought-iron gates which opened into the drive. At any minute now, Hope Connell would walk through them.

He could hear Agatha singing in a distant room. His sister enjoyed entertaining, and for some reason tonight's small dinner party filled her with pleasurable anticipation. It was nice of her, he thought, to invite the Connell girls, and pretended to himself that as far as he was concerned the evening held no special significance.

And yet he watched the wrought-iron gates through which Hope Connell would enter.

Agatha's singing had stopped. A moment later her footsteps sounded outside the door. 'I'm in here!' he called. 'In the study. Come and see the sunset. It is magnificent tonight.'

She saw the proud outline of his features etched against the evening light and her heart, as always, stirred at the sight of him. Agatha hid her deep affection for her brother beneath a guise of light-hearted banter. Not for the world would she have him—or anyone—suspect the depth of her love and pride. Doting sisters, she thought, were as bad as doting mothers.

Phillip said: 'You seem excited tonight Agatha. Why? What's so special about this dinner party?'

'Nothing!' Her voice was briskly evasive. He knew that tone of old, and regarded her suspiciously. 'Don't look at me like that, Phillip!' she chided. 'I'm only anxious that the evening should be a success.'

'Why shouldn't it be?'

She opened her mouth to speak, then closed it abruptly. Phillip regarded her with brotherly affection and said: 'What you need is a drink, old girl. Come along and I'll mix you one.'

They turned their backs upon the sunset and went down to the long drawing-room on the ground floor. Soft lamplight threw into delicate relief the gilt-edged paneling of the walls, the faded rugs, the warm chintz and mellow paintings. It was a charming, gracious room and, thought Agatha frankly, it needed a charming, gracious young woman to play hostess here. What she herself wanted, in the secret places of her heart, was a comfortable little cottage high up on the cliffs above the Old Town; a cottage where she could relax and put her feet up, paint when she felt so inclined, grow a few vegetables and a few flowers, and invite only the friends she really wanted to see. I was born to be an old maid, she thought without rancor, and I'd like to have the chance of enjoying that blissful state. Aloud she said abruptly: 'I wish you would marry, Phillip.'

He stared at her, his hands arrested in action. Then, with a laugh, he filled her glass and held it toward her.

'I was right, Agatha. What you need *is* a drink!'

She felt as cross as a mother toward a small pugnacious boy.

'I mean it, Phillip. You're too set in your ways, too comfortable and well looked after. What would you do if I wasn't here to play housekeeper?'

'Hire one.' He grinned, and raised his glass in a mock toast. 'But here's to the unpaid one I've already got!'

She wanted to throw something at him. She wanted to accuse him of selfishness and stodginess, but could not because he was neither of those things. He was simply a brilliant man devoted to his work.

'And what prompts such an announcement?' her brother asked.

She jerked to awareness.

'What announcement?'

'That I should marry.'

She regarded him frankly.

'Simply that you should. You're young and virile and strong. You're nice, too.' Her amiable face creased with humor. 'I suppose that sounds funny, coming from a sister. But I'm fond of you, Phillip.' She took another sip. 'Don't let's get sentimental!' She laughed, and he laughed with her.

All the same, he was interested. It was the first time his sister had ever referred to matrimony, to his personal and private life. Agatha, bless her, was always completely detached. She never interfered. She ran the old house efficiently and looked after him well.

'That's the trouble,' he mused.

'What is?'

'That you look after me too well . . .'

'I can always slack off!' she warned.

'Not you. It isn't in your nature to slack off.

But perhaps it is your capable management which has kept me a bachelor so long.'

He was being evasive, and they both knew it. It was Felicity who had made a bachelor of Phillip, and in his heart he knew that, too. What he should have done, when Felicity married her wealthy Marcus, was to have married someone else. Only he never looked at anyone else. Work had been his refuge. Work could always be a man's refuge.

Agatha said tentatively: 'All the same, Phillip—why don't you?'

'Marry, you mean? My dear woman, are you seriously trying to make me?'

'I'd like to be an aunt!' she retorted lightly.

'And you consider that reason enough for your brother to find a wife?'

Still his voice was light and bantering and amused. He wasn't considering the thing seriously. Or did he adopt that attitude merely because the subject was, after all, hidden in the deep recesses of his heart? A shiver of fear touched his sister. Was he really thinking of Felicity? Would he really marry her, given the opportunity?

She turned aside. Her movements were restless, a complete contrast with her normal serenity. Something was wrong with Agatha tonight. Phillip's shrewd eyes observed her quietly. Her strong, capable hands pulled the curtain ropes and sent the wide brocades sweeping across the bay, shutting out the advancing night. 'They should be here soon,' she said. 'I'm glad the Connell girls are coming. I like them.'

'Yes,' he agreed. 'They are a charming trio.'

'D'you know something, Phillip? I believe Michael Shearing is falling in love with the little blind one, Charity.'

He was surprised—and pleased. Michael's crust of cynicism needed stripping from his vulnerable heart. Beneath lay kindness and a deep capacity for loving. He had idolized his mother as a child. A boy with less affection would have weathered that separation more ably, he reflected. From one extreme to another went Michael Shearing—from devotion to hatred. But underneath he remained the same; fundamentally his heart was unchanged.

'Are you sure of this, Agatha?'

'Pretty sure. And pleased. Aren't you?'

Phillip's serious face smiled gently. 'If it really is true, yes. And if something comes of it. She's a sweet child. And right for him, I should say. Michael needs to love someone who has accepted suffering.'

'Poor Michael,' Agatha whispered. 'If I could wipe the disillusion from his heart, I should be thankful.'

'I doubt if that can ever be erased. He adored his mother and she let him down—'

'But *did* she?' Agatha cried. 'How do we *know* she did?'

'My dear girl, she left Michael and his father for another man. If *that* isn't letting a child down, what is?'

'People make mistakes—and suffer for them,' Agatha pleaded. 'Somehow I could never regard Edwina Shearing as a bad or a selfish woman. And who are we to judge another person's wrong? When people are desperately unhappy, they do things which they themselves would normally condemn. We are all capable of it—yes, you and I and the next person, Phillip! If Edwina could only have turned to someone . . .!'

'She had her husband. She turned away from him.'

'Then he must have made her very unhappy,' Agatha declared vigorously. 'So unhappy that, rather than let her wretchedness pervade their home, she went away. How do you know she didn't do that in the vain hope that her child would not be caught in the web of her unhappiness? Children sense more than we grown-ups realize. A child devoted to a parent knows when that parent is unhappy, no matter how valiantly it is concealed.'

'All that is true,' Phillip conceded, 'but in Edwina Shearing's case you overlook one thing. She left her husband to marry someone else.'

Agatha took a deep breath.

'But she didn't, Phillip. She didn't marry anyone else. She's still Edwina Shearing and she's here in Highcliffe—and, what's more, she is coming to this house tonight.'

CHAPTER TWELVE

The sound of wheels on gravel heralded the arrival of their first guests.

It was Charles Willstack, who had brought the Connell girls in his rip-roaring sports car. Beside him—close beside him, for the accommodation was cramped—sat Faith, her hair blown into a dark cloud about her head. In the light from the house he turned and looked at her. 'You look like a Valkyrie, Faith, riding against the wind . . .' She laughed, that rare sweet sound which delighted him, and answered lightly: 'I feel like one!'

Hope looked at her sister with interest. Was this the calm, restrained Faith who always looked immaculate and well-groomed, who took life so seriously? She had ridden in this open sports car all the way up from the hospital as if frankly enjoying it. They had all enjoyed it. Charity, sitting upon Hope's knee, had laughed her delight, feeling the cold night wind stream through her hair. Charity's heart was light this evening—light with expectation, for Michael was to be part of it, and whenever she thought of Michael she was aware of a quickening of gladness, a deep tenderness springing like a fountain within her.

Hope, too, felt an excitement within her. It was by now a familiar sensation, for it assailed her whenever Phillip Trent was due in Luke's ward. Today it had been steadily increasing. From her earliest childhood she had been aware of the old white house upon Beacon Hill. Sometimes she had peeped through the wrought-iron gates, as if at the castle of her dreams. That, she thought, was *home*—home as every woman dreamed of it. Gentle and mellow and enduring. A house which would enfold you as a mother enfolds a child in her arms.

She had never dreamed that she would enter it, yet now here she was—standing at the front door. The magic gates had opened and admitted her, and soon the heavy oak door would open too, and she would walk into the home of the man she loved.

The door opened and light spilled out into the porch. Agatha's kindly face greeted them, her smile warm and generous and welcoming. She was never so happy as when young people gathered about her, and she surveyed them now—Hope with her flame of bright hair, her honest eyes, her generous mouth, and Faith, with her dark beauty blossoming like some night-scented plant, and Charity, gentle as moonlight, and as clear, with that ethereal loveliness which seemed to emanate from her soul.

The woman's plump arms stretched out to greet them. 'Come in!' she cried. 'Welcome, all of you!' And into the wide hall they came, into the house which Agatha's sincerity and Phillip's stability made into a thing of comfort and endurance. There was an atmosphere of home about the place which had nothing to do with its structure or design. The Trent family had always lived here, and always would—a visitor was aware of that the moment they entered. Hope felt its friendliness enfold her like a cloak.

And then Phillip was before her, holding out a welcoming hand, smiling down at her in his serious, endearing fashion. For a fleeting moment she recalled her first impression of him—grim, forbidding, intense. Now she wondered how she could ever have regarded him so. Underlying his seriousness was his sisters' sincerity and a depth of character which was as steady as a rock.

Agatha took the girls upstairs. Faith said: 'What a lovely house, Miss Trent!' and Agatha warmed to the united echo from the other two. There was no envy in their voices, merely frank appreciation and delight. To these girls, who had never had a home, the house on Beacon Hill was the epitome of their dreams. Charity's sensitive hand touched the banisters. She said: 'How I love the sheen on mahogany! This *is* mahogany, isn't it? Oak is warm and stolid, and walnut satiny and rich, and mahogany a combination of all!'

'Then that is something you share with Michael,' Agatha told her. 'He always admires this staircase. I tell him the polish on the rail is due to the seat of his pants, as a boy. He never could resist sliding down it!' Leading the way to her bedroom, she continued conversationally: 'He should be here any minute now. I thought you might all come together.'

'Doctor Willstack brought us,' Faith said. 'Doctor Shearing had a call at half past five, which delayed him slightly. Otherwise he would have brought Charity. We'll divide between the two cars going home.'

Faith's voice had a new lightness in it, a new vivacity. Not only Hope observed the subtle change in her sister, but Charity also, who was particularly sensitive to the nuances of a person's voice. Faith's had always been like a gentle benediction; now the benediction was set to music and was infinitely beautiful. Could such a change really be due merely to a less restrained atmosphere in the laboratory?

'Charles didn't mind piling us all in,' Hope said as she smoothed her titian hair. 'He's a good-natured man—like a tonic at St. Bede's.'

Her warm amber eyes glanced swiftly at her sister, but Faith's betrayed nothing. At any rate, thought Hope with inner amusement, she doesn't deny the fact!

Hope smiled inwardly and followed the

others downstairs. Charles, in the mellow hall below, glanced up at their approach, and Phillip, beside him, did likewise. Both men were stirred by the sight of the three girls—so alike, yet so unalike, coming down the wide curving staircase toward them. There was a strange significance about the moment, as if a curtain were going up, revealing characters who were important and essential to both of them.

Phillip was glad that Agatha had invited Charles Willstack. They rarely met at the hospital, and from their first meeting he had liked the man. Agatha had invited him as a stopgap for old Colonel Shearing—a very acceptable stopgap, thought Phillip with gratitude. He pitied Michael's father, but disliked his taciturnity and bitterness.

From the moment the girls appeared upon the staircase, the evening promised to be enjoyable for Phillip. He could not tell why, but he was aware of it at once, as if a friendly hand laid a blessing upon them all. He poured sherry and smiled at Hope as they raised their glasses, and felt again the warm response to her which he had felt before. He recalled that moment in the operating theatre, when her tender heart had been so touched by old Mrs. Tompkins. So often theatre nurses became immune to suffering, but here was one nurse who would be forever moved by it. He liked her for that.

Beneath the hum of conversation, he watched her. She was admiring a Sheraton screen which had belonged to Agatha's godmother. They were getting along well together, his sister and the staff nurse from Luke's. They were deep in conversation, as if already life-long friends. The gap in their ages seemed to make no difference. Of course Agatha liked young people. Phillip reminded himself of that fact, squashing the unbidden thought that even a lifetime had never brought any friendship between Agatha and Felicity.

There came the sound of wheels on gravel again, and there was Michael, standing on the old porch, smiling at the couple who had been his lifelong friends. His eyes went beyond them to the quiet figure of Charity, standing in the warm shadows of the hall. She was looking toward him, her sightless eyes alight with pleasure, and in the depths of Michael's lonely heart he felt a swift upsurge of happiness, a floodtide of tenderness. He realized then that he had been waiting for this moment all day.

'Sufficient unto the hour is the happiness thereof,' parodied a contented corner of his mind. He would not go beyond that. He would not analyze or question. He would not even resist. Why the sight of Charity should fill him with such peace he could not tell. It was not because she was a woman, of course, or because he was in any way attracted by her. It was simply because, inexplicably, he felt a sense of communion with her, and that was enough. He sought no further explanation.

'I'm taking you home—you know that, don't you?' he said in a brief moment of isolation, and she smiled her sweet smile, thanking him politely. He let his eyes rest upon her with undisguised pleasure, thinking tenderly that one of the advantages of Charity's blindness was the fact that he had no need to conceal his glance from her. He could study her if he wished, without her knowledge.

But he was wrong. She felt his glance. She knew that he watched her. Deep color flooded her face and she turned away, embarrassed and shy. Both were unfamiliar emotions to her, for never before had she been conscious of herself. Yet now the dark glance of this young doctor penetrated to her heart. She felt acutely aware of his nearness, and most disturbingly aware of her own reactions to him.

Agatha glanced at her watch. Now she was feeling nervous—an unfamiliar sensation to one of her placid temperament. She prayed devoutly that nothing would go wrong this evening. Michael seemed happy, which augured well. She glanced across at him, observing his deep interest in Charity, and over his shoulder met the reassuring glance of her brother. 'Don't worry,' said Phillip's calm grey eyes. 'What is to be, will be—and I'm here to help, old girl . . .'

They were all gathered now—all but Edwina Shearing, who had refused Agatha's offer of transportation. 'I'll enjoy the walk, Agatha. I remember the way quite well.' Perhaps she needed the fresh air and exercise, Agatha thought sympathetically, to bolster her courage. Perhaps stepping back into the past, even into the house of old friends, was an ordeal. For this reason Agatha had said nothing about bringing her face to face with Michael. 'Come and have a meal with us, Edwina.' That was all she had said, fearing that if she revealed more Edwina herself might choose to stay away.

Hope and Phillip were laughing at something Charles Willstack was saying. Beside them, Faith smiled quietly, her lips gradually parting upon laughter. Slightly detached were Charity and Michael, absorbed in one another. Agatha glanced about the hall, her heart warming to the picture they all made against the mellow old paneling. They were a handsome sextet, she thought fondly. Three pairs, all well matched . . .

And into her thoughts cut the shrill peal of the front door bell.

She saw Phillip's eyes seek hers.

He moved across the hall and reached her side just as she opened the door and looked into the arrogant, challenging face of Felicity.

CHAPTER THIRTEEN

Felicity said gaily: 'Hello, there! I rang twice and no one seemed to hear. Is there a party on? Sorry if I intrude . . .'

She was angry, and Agatha knew it. Felicity would never forgive her for excluding her from any party. She would regard it as a deliberate slight and nurse her resentment indefinitely, finally assuaging it, no matter how long she had to wait, by retaliating in some way. Phillip didn't realize that, of course. Men never did. A wave of exasperation surged through Agatha and she shut the door with a hollow little slam.

Felicity glanced over her shoulder, raised mocking eyebrows and murmured: 'Sorry, Agatha darling—you should have warned me to keep away!'

It was right at that moment that Agatha realized everything was to go wrong. Happy anticipation subsided like a pricked balloon. It was as if, with Felicity's coming, fate stepped in and took a hand—a malicious hand. And before it Agatha herself was powerless.

Phillip said: 'I was going to call you, Felicity—'

'Darling, you always say that!' She reached up and kissed him, lightly but possessively, upon the tip of his chin.

Agatha said with forced amiability: 'You'll

have a drink, Felicity?'

'A cocktail, please, Phillip,' Felicity ordered, ignoring Agatha completely.

Not until then did she glance round the company, and something in her reaction communicated itself to Agatha. She followed Felicity's eyes and discovered that they were fixed in a cold, calculating stare upon the frank young face of Hope Connell. And, for some reason, her anger deepened and hardened.

'Let me introduce you,' said Agatha quietly and, with instinctive tact, presented Doctor Wilistack first. She knew Felicity's liking for the opposite sex, and Charles was undeniably handsome, undeniably attractive. Felicity's feline glance encompassed him from head to foot, approved, accepted . . . and finally she smiled. She turned the full force of her radiance upon him, to which Charles showed remarkable resistance.

'And Miss Connell,' said Agatha. 'Miss Faith Connell, Doctor Willstack's assistant . . .'

'A female pathologist!' Felicity trilled. 'How very brainy you must be, Miss Connell . . .' A regular blue-stocking, in fact, said her unfinished sentence.

Faith's reaction was surprising—and, to Charles, quite delightful. She burst out laughing. Her lovely mouth parted upon even white teeth and amusement bubbled up like a fountain from her heart. 'I always think the word "brainy" has a sort of suet-pudding sound!' she chuckled, and at once everyone, as if relieved from tension, laughed, too.

'Anything less like a suet-pudding than my assistant it would be hard to find,' said Charles to Felicity. But he was not looking at her. He was not even interested in her. He was looking at no one but Faith. Beneath his breath he said: 'I knew you could do it! I've been waiting for it!'

'For what?' asked Faith.

'For a spontaneous burst of gaiety, a peep out of your shell . . .'

Her eyes faltered and looked away.

She followed Felicity's progress about the room. 'She's very beautiful, isn't she?' she said, and Charles—his eyes still upon her face—murmured: 'Very. I have always thought so.' She turned and looked at him, realized the meaning behind his words, and felt a deep tide of color surge to her face. She wished she did not blush so easily, quite unaware of the delight her betrayal gave Charles.

Felicity paused before Hope. Phillip, placing a glass in her exquisitely manicured hand, said: 'Let me introduce Nurse Connell, Felicity—' but before he could go further Felicity said coolly: 'We've already met. You are nursing my sister, aren't you?'

'I was,' Hope admitted.

'Was?' Felicity echoed.

'I mean that it isn't necessary any more. She's well enough to go home, as I expect you've heard.'

Felicity gave a short laugh.

'I certainly have. Some upstart of a doctor has discharged her, I understand.'

'I,' said Michael's quiet voice, 'am the upstart.'

Slowly, Felicity turned. No one could move with such grace as she, nor with such calculated charm. If she was disturbed by the challenging note in Michael's voice, she gave no sign, but her eyes smoldered.

Slowly and resentfully she turned and surveyed young Doctor Shearing, and at once her face relaxed into a disarming smile. 'Why,' she said, 'if it isn't Colonel Shearing's son! We met once—remember?'

Michael didn't, or didn't want to. His reaction was so plain that the smile was wiped from Felicity's face like a child's picture from a slate. She shrugged, waved a negligent hand, and said: 'Oh, well, what does it matter? One meets so many . . .! As for that kid sister of mine, I couldn't care less! But watch out for dear Mamma! She's after your blood!'

'So I understand,' said Michael evenly.

Phillip, determined to rescue the moment from complete disaster, said: 'Drink up, Felicity . . .' He knew how mellow she could become on a few cocktails, and right at this moment even that was preferable to her icy humor.

But once more a voice arrested Felicity—

this time a girl's voice, sweet and clear as a bell.

'What do you mean?' it asked. 'Why should your mother be after Michael's blood?'

It was that unusual girl standing beside the doctor—unmistakably another Connell, and pretty in a Dresden-china sort of way. There was something about her steady, unblinking gaze that disturbed even Felicity's composure. For once, she felt uncomfortable—almost afraid. She shrugged again and said lightly: 'Oh—nothing. It doesn't matter, anyway.'

'But it does,' the girl persisted. 'If your sister is Miss Ransom—I'm right, aren't!?—I can uphold Doctor Shearing's opinion. She doesn't even need further treatment from me.'

'In that case,' Phillip put in with calm assurance, 'Caroline must certainly be well enough to go home, Felicity, Miss Connell is St. Bede's physiotherapist. We all think the world of her, don't we, Michael?' And he smiled in his strong, gentle fashion at the two young people.

Felicity yawned. 'My dear Phillip, what does it matter? Not to me, anyway, only to Mother. But you know what an idiot she is! No one should say her baby is well until she gives the word! Instead, a junior physician—you *are* a junior, aren't you, Doctor?—takes it upon himself to dismiss our little Caroline! That was very foolish of you, Doctor Shearing. You'll find out.'

Agatha thought: I hate Felicity. I don't dislike her—I really hate her. And if I have her as a sister-in-law I shall hate her even more . . . Why doesn't she go? What did she come for, anyway? She's offered no excuse.

As if sensing her thoughts, Felicity did so now.

'Phillip,' she said calmly, 'are you ready?'

'Ready?' he echoed, his fine brows drawing together in a puzzled line. 'For what, Felicity?'

She gave a gay tinkle of a laugh. 'Men!' she sighed in mock despair. 'Have they all such bad memories, or is it merely a characteristic of the medical profession?'

She surveyed Phillip's baffled glance with tender amusement. 'Darling, had you *really* forgotten our dinner date?'

There was a brief, stony little silence, broken by Phillip's strong voice saying in disbelief: 'We had no date for dinner tonight, surely?'

Felicity's smile became more dazzling.

'Now that,' she trilled, 'is just about the most unflattering comment any man can make to any woman! I excuse it only because I know how terribly overworked you are, Phillip. But of course we had a date, darling—at the Marine Grill, at seven-thirty. I came to collect you because I know you've had a tiring day and mightn't feel like driving . . .'

'I'm sorry, Felicity,' he answered steadily; 'there must be some mistake.'

Her eyes hardened. Her mouth became more determined. 'No mistake,' she said softly, clearly, in a tone which brooked no argument. 'There's a table booked in your name for seven-thirty, Phillip.'

For a long moment he stared at her. It was a mistake, and he knew it, but she placed him in an awkward situation.

He said again: 'I'm sorry, Felicity—there must be some mistake.'

Agatha took a deep breath. There was no table booked at the Marine, of course, but the whole situation could be eased by inviting her to stay.

Agatha was cornered even more than her brother, who sometimes had a way of simply refusing to be cornered. At this moment he was preparing to dig his heels in, just as he had done as a small boy, making the atmosphere embarrassing for their guests and painful for herself as hostess. No, thought Agatha wretchedly, there *is* nothing else to be done . . .

She heard her own voice say calmly: 'Why not cancel the table at the Marine, Phillip? Won't you dine with us here, Felicity?'

Felicity smiled. She had won. And at once the tension in the atmosphere vanished. So, too, did the promise of an enjoyable evening. There wasn't a person in the room who did not feel a sudden chill.

And right at that moment Edwina Shearing arrived.

CHAPTER FOURTEEN

Agatha had hustled away to order an extra cover to be laid for dinner. Felicity had trailed upstairs to leave her coat in Agatha's bedroom. 'Don't trouble to come with me, Agatha—I know my way!' She had thrown the remark casually over her shoulder, but her glance slid across to Hope, as if to direct its significance straight at her. She was emphasizing her familiarity with this house, suggesting that she was already part of it.

Quite suddenly, Hope wanted to take herself away from this house in which, quite obviously, she could not hope to fit. She wondered now why she had felt a sense of welcome, a sense of 'belonging' when first she entered—such a feeling could only have been imaginary, the result of wishful thinking on her part. She had dreamed of a home like this all her life—so, no doubt, had her sisters—but even as a guest, she was really out of place.

She was aware that Phillip, standing nearby, said: 'Excuse me—' and walked across the wide hall toward the front door. She heard Michael say to Charity: 'And what does Mustard do when you step out for an evening without him?' His voice was light and happy, vastly different from the abrupt, almost saturnine voice the nursing staff heard at the hospital. Forgetting herself with characteristic promptitude, Hope looked across at him. He's really awfully nice, she thought. I like him. I wonder if shyness is the reason for that abrupt manner in the wards? It might be just a cover-up, as Charity says. She is so much more perceptive than the rest of us . . .

Phillip was opening the front door. Light from the porch spilled into the softly lit hall like a spotlight upon a stage, silhouetting the figure of a woman outside. Something about the woman's stillness arrested Hope—a sort of 'waiting' stillness as if, for a long, long time, she had been keeping silence with life, letting it do with her what it willed. Why she gave this impression Hope could not imagine, for at this distance she could not even see the woman's face.

She heard Charity's happy voice say to Michael: 'Oh, he thoroughly enjoys himself in the kitchen, being made a fuss of by the domestic staff and spoiled with tid-bits!'

Michael stood with his back to the door, his interest focused solely upon Charity. Charles and Faith were deep in conversation. None but Hope had observed the new arrival. She saw Phillip stretch out a welcoming hand.

He was drawing the woman into the hall. He was closing the door and, with his hand beneath her elbow, bringing her across. Now Hope could see the newcomer more clearly she observed the rather shabby suit, once well-tailored and expensive, obviously a relic of better days, and the general air of fortitude about her. Once upon a time she had been lovely; now tiredness had overtaken her, leaving her with only the remnants of former good looks. Yet there was a sort of patient serenity about her which held a grace of its own.

Agatha came bustling back from the dining-room. She stood still abruptly, then hurried forward. 'Edwina!' she said. 'How nice to see you!' And Michael, his back still toward them, was suddenly tense.

The woman was taking Agatha's hand. Agatha placed her free one upon her shoulder, reached forward and kissed her upon the cheek. Hope could not understand why the newcomer's eyes should fill with tears.

'Thank you, Agatha.' That was all she said, but her voice echoed clearly in the vaulted hall, and it was soft and musical and lovely.

Charity said with an air of pleased surprise: 'Why, I know that voice! It belongs to my friend from the park!'

And Michael remained quite still, his back turned. Something about his silence communicated itself to Charity, and she said swiftly: 'Michael—is anything the matter?'

'Nothing,' he said abruptly, and turned.

Edwina Shearing stood between Phillip and his sister, but she was not even aware of their nearness. She was aware of nothing—neither the faces around her, nor the sudden silence—nothing but the dark, shocked face of the young man whose features were unmistakably those she had carried in her memory all these years. She made no movement, gave no sign. For a long moment they stood thus, looking at one another, and as if silenced by some warning signal the rest of the company were still, surrendering the moment to them. Then Phillip spoke.

'Michael . . .' he said gently.

That was all, but in it was understanding and pleading and something more—something intimate and personal, meant for him alone. But Charity heard it. She heard the underlying sympathy linked with a note of challenge, as if one man called to the other to stand fast, to believe, and to help.

She heard more. She heard Michael's swift in-drawn breath—a breath which betrayed so much: shock and fear and anger, all inextricably mixed with pain. And then silence again.

Agatha's voice spoke next. 'Michael,' she said, clutching desperately at a calmness she did not feel, 'Michael, this is—'

And the old, embittered voice which Charity had hoped never to hear again answered tautly: 'You don't have to tell me, Agatha. I know.'

It was then that he did a terrible, an unforgivable thing. He turned his back upon them all and walked out of Phillip Trent's house.

'Well, well!' said a brittle voice from above. 'That was a pretty little scene!'

It was, thought Agatha beneath the confusion of her distress, typical of Felicity. None but she could throw so tactless a remark into a difficult moment and get away with it. Yet, in a way, her arrival was merciful, releasing a spring of tension in the atmosphere. One could almost hear it snap.

Phillip said: 'Edwina, may I present Mrs. Drake? Felicity—Mrs. Shearing.'

'Shearing?' echoed Felicity, eyebrows raised. 'Any relation to Michael Shearing, by any chance?'

Edwina took a deep breath.

'Yes,' she said. 'His mother.'

It wasn't Felicity's reaction which disturbed her, but the reaction of someone standing by. It was imperceptible, but definite; the merest reflection of surprise swiftly concealed. Edwina felt Felicity's brief handshake and cool appraisal. Instinctively, she turned away and saw the beautiful, sightless eyes of Charity Connell looking toward her.

Nothing could have steadied Edwina's shaken heart more than the calm serenity of this girl. She felt an uptide of relief envelop her spirit. Charity smiled and said: 'I thought I recognized your voice—' and held out her hands, both of them, in welcome.

'You two know each other, don't you?' Phillip said, feeling obscurely thankful that he could lead Edwina away from Felicity's calculating glance.

'We know each other well!' Charity said gaily. 'We are almost old friends by now!'

She was careful to make her voice particularly warm, particularly welcoming. Michael's abrupt departure, his transition from happiness to anger, had shocked her deeply, but since some instinct told her that ungraciousness was alien to his nature, she sensed at once that the cause of his behavior was unexpected and disturbing. Michael might be abrupt, bitter and rebellious, but he was too fond of the Trents to behave in such a manner unless he had been shocked out of self-control.

Now, for the first time, Charity was beginning to glimpse the dark well of unhappiness in which he floundered. Hitherto she had merely sensed it. She had guessed at some secret hurt, some distant disillusion, but until this moment had had no idea as to its cause. Behind the dark screen of her eyes she hid her thoughts and speculations—hid, too, her own personal surprise.

Agatha, still trying to steady an evening which threatened to topple altogether, now announced that dinner was served. Felicity smiled at her mockingly and murmured: 'What a pity you troubled to lay an extra cover, dear—it won't be needed after all!' Her low voice, as she intended, reached no one but Agatha, who turned without a word and led the way into the dining-room.

Felicity linked her arm in Phillip's and drew him slightly away from the little procession. 'My dear,' she whispered, 'whatever possessed Agatha to stage this little affair? Rather tactless, wasn't it? Is that woman really the errant Mrs. Shearing?'

Phillip looked down at her. For the first time that he could remember, he was not stirred by her loveliness. Instead, he was embarrassed. Just in front of them walked Hope Connell, with her soft warm eyes and tender mouth. He could not imagine so tender a mouth producing the brittle observation which Felicity had thrown from the top of the stairs. What was the matter with Felicity tonight? What had got into her? She wasn't herself at all.

He said quietly: 'Both Agatha and I were glad to welcome Edwina to our house. Let's leave it at that, shall we?'

Felicity gave a mock shudder, looked up at him with melting eyes, clung a little more tightly to his arm and pleaded: 'Darling—don't look so cross!'

She was hard to resist when she put on that pleading little act. Unwillingly, he smiled, wondering why the evening had gone wrong from the moment of Felicity's arrival. Prior to that it held a promise of happiness—an unreliable promise, of course. He shouldn't have trusted it, knowing of the unfortunate meeting his sister had planned. All the same, he felt, quite illogically, that it *might* have worked if only some fantastic quirk of fate had not intervened.

To change the subject he said: 'As for our dinner date, you minx, you know quite well we had none tonight.'

She screwed up her entrancing nose provocatively, 'Ring up the Marine Grill and find out!' she chuckled. Then, with the swift transition from gaiety to intimacy at which she was so adept, she murmured: 'Darling, can you blame me? I was feeling blue, and no one can cure me of the blues so well as you. Besides, I thought after a long day in town you'd enjoy a *tête-à-tête* meal with me—even in a public dining-room! I'd no idea Agatha had other plans.' She pouted prettily. 'Sorry if I butted in!'

CHAPTER FIFTEEN

Matron sat alone in her charming sitting-room. Soon John Benham would be arriving for tea—he always came on Sunday afternoon. So, too, did 'her three girls,' either singly or together. Hope, she knew, was on duty today, so that would be one guest less, but Faith and

Charity would probably drop in. Sometimes they all went to vespers together; then she and John Benham would come back here, sit beside the fire and chat. It was a ritual which had been going on for years.

When Matron paused to count just how many years, it gave her quite a shock. She and John seemed part and parcel of St. Bede's Hospital now. 'We're the original foundation stones!' John would laugh, but he was as proud of the fact as she. They would grow old together in the hospital's service. They had always been together. Once upon a time it had seemed that they would be together in other ways, too, not merely as pillars of the hospital.

Matron jerked her mind away from the thought. She had put it aside so long ago that it seemed silly to take it out now, dust it, and sigh over it. She had made her choice and she had not regretted it. Had John? That she would never know.

She heard a sound outside the door, a padding, shuffling sound which was familiar—the sound of Mustard's paws guiding his mistress to the familiar room. He knew every curve of the passage which led through the residents' quarters to this door. She wanted to jump up and open the door for them, but knowing Charity's dislike of help, she refrained.

The handle turned and Charity's clear voice called: 'May I come in?'

'By all means, my dear, I'm delighted to see you.'

'I've come early—do you mind?' She stooped, released Mustard's collar, and walked confidently across to the fire. This room was almost as familiar to her as the one over in the nurses' home. Matron rarely moved the furniture about, and never without warning her beforehand, telling her just where everything was to be placed. Sometimes Charity even made suggestions about altering the arrangement. She said it was fun to plan the furnishing of rooms and that if only she'd been able to see colors she would have gone in for interior decoration. But she said it without any wistful regrets, for she enjoyed life even without color.

That was why the change in her today was so noticeable. For the first time in her life Matron saw the happiness in Charity's eyes dulled and obscured.

She said gently: 'Something is wrong, my dear. I hope you have come early to tell me about it.'

She heard the almost imperceptible sound of a suppressed sob—a sound which disturbed her so deeply that her maternal hands reached out to the girl swiftly. Even so, in childhood, had they reached toward the blind girl, guiding her uncertain steps, protecting her from harm. With the growth of her independence physical help had become unnecessary, but still Charity turned to her—as now—when in need of assurance or help. It had been Matron's suggestion that Charity should study physiotherapy; the girl was intelligent and gifted with an additional sensitivity of her hands. That had been the first step in assuring her complete independence, and from then on she had forged ahead. Acquiring a guide dog had been an additional help, but the success had been Charity's own, the result of her courage, her determination, and her complete lack of self-pity.

Matron urged her into a chair, gently. 'Tell me—' she said, and waited while the girl regained her control.

'It's silly of me to care,' Charity whispered. 'But I do—oh, I *do!* I knew he was bitter, but I thought it was merely a disguise for his heart. I didn't believe he was really hard! But now I know he is . . .'

Her hands reached out blindly, seeking comfort and help. Swiftly, the older woman encompassed them in her own, saying nothing, just waiting.

'I mean Michael—' Charity whispered.

'I thought you did, my dear. What has he done now?'

'It's more a case of what he has *not* done!'

'Meaning?' Matron urged gently.

'Meaning that he turned his back upon someone—someone who needed him—'

'A patient?' demanded Matron, her

professional conscience stirred.

'No! Oh, no! He is too good a doctor to reject a patient!' Charity's tender mouth curved ruefully. 'Sometimes I think they mean more to him than people—people in his own life, I mean.'

'This was someone in his own life?'

'His mother.'

'But I thought she had gone out of his life!'

'She has come back. And she's sweet—so sweet. But Michael turned his back upon her—just like that—the moment he set eyes upon her, and walked away.'

'Well,' said Matron carefully, 'perhaps that was understandable, especially if he was unprepared. Shock can make people react in unpredictable ways. And I've always heard—not that I know the true story, of course—that his mother deserted him.'

Charity's gentle face was creased with anxiety and doubt.

'But I can't believe that! It just doesn't seem *like* her. I've known her for quite a time, and she has always been so kind and understanding and human. She runs a little café in the park—you know I exercise Mustard there and stop for tea sometimes—'

'Edwina Shearing—no, that isn't her name, of course—*Edwina* running a little café in the park! My dear, you must be mistaken.'

'No—I'm not. And her name is still Shearing. And Agatha Trent met her and invited her to dine last night.'

'And Michael was there—and didn't know she was coming?'

'Yes.'

'And ran away?'

'I suppose you could call it that,' Charity said sadly.

'Do you call it that? I don't. It was merely a sort of defense mechanism going up. Oh, I know the young man is bitter—everyone knows that—but bitterness, I always think, is merely a disguise for deeper unhappiness. Shock prompted his action, Charity—not hardness of heart.'

'Are you sure of that?' the girl asked eagerly, turning her sightless eyes toward her with desperate entreaty. 'Oh, if that were true!'

'Well,' said Matron briskly, 'let's try to view it logically. Don't you think indifference would have produced an entirely different reaction?'

'You mean—if he didn't care he wouldn't have turned away?'

'Precisely.'

Charity's face became suddenly radiant with hope. Matron looked at her and smiled.

'Emotion struck deeply, my dear, so, instinctively, he retreated. But when shock passed, reason would begin to assert itself. You see if I am not right. If Michael had been able to meet his mother without any reaction at all, you'd have had cause to believe him hard and unfeeling.'

Charity took a deep breath and smiled.

'That's better!' said Matron gently. 'You know, Charity, I've suspected all along that young Doctor Shearing was intensely vulnerable—more capable of feeling than many people who call themselves "sensitive."' She studied the girl for a long moment, than said softly. 'Remember that, Charity. Remember it and be glad of it. It is good to love someone who really has a heart.'

The pathological laboratory was situated at the top of the main hospital block, with unshielded skylights and vast windows to admit the maximum amount of light. The sun shone brilliantly upon Faith's bowed head, and as Doctor Willstack entered the following morning he paused momentarily, watching her. The sheen upon her dark hair reminded him of the petals of a black tulip—as satin-smooth and as rich. He thought spontaneously: Some day, when I have a home of my own, I'll have a bed of black tulips in the garden, to remind me of her . . .

But he knew that he really wanted no home that was not her home, too. He seemed to have known this for a long time and was surprised that the realization should only come to him now. He had been aware of her attraction, of course, right from that challenging moment of their first meeting. He had determined then to break down her defenses and invade the private citadel of her heart, but only because her reserve was provoking to a man of his temperament.

Or so he believed. Now he knew that it went deeper, this desire of his. He had begun to suspect it on Saturday evening, at the Trents' house, when the sweet concern upon her face had revealed the true depths of her compassionate heart. Her concern had been for Charity, so obviously stunned by Michael Shearing's abrupt departure. Faith had watched her as a mother would watch a child, powerless to protect it from hurt, and when the blind girl had rallied and held out welcoming hands to Michael's mother, Faith's tender mouth had smiled with relief and pride.

Was it then that he had realized the depths of his love for her, or had it been growing, like a secret flower, reaching full bloom at that moment?

What matter? The truth held a wonder and a glory which was beyond analysis. There had been women in his life before, but none had affected him as this girl did; none had mattered as she mattered. He thought it impossible that he could ever mean the same to her. Overcoming her resistance, conquering her disapproval of him, did not amount to much—not, at least, in comparison with his own love.

He closed the door, and she turned at the sound. Her smile was lovely—like a melody, he thought, which would haunt him forever. He crossed to her work table and looked down at the segments she was mounting. They were beautifully cut and he said so, complimenting her in a matter-of-fact voice. She seemed pleased by his approval, but he suspected that she would have been more pleased by the approval of her former chief.

He felt unaccountably depressed—an unfamiliar feeling to a man of his temperament. She glanced at him swiftly, sensing his mood. She was becoming more and more aware of the pathologist as each day passed—a fact which surprised her. She didn't even resent him any more—that surprised her, too. The laboratory ran as well, if not better, than before, and the atmosphere was certainly a much happier one, easier to work in. The tempo had speeded up and their working output with it. No longer did it proceed at a slow, steady pace. A vitality had come into it, and the vitality emanated from this man.

But she was aware of him not only as an efficient pathologist—she was aware of him as a man, also, especially since Saturday night. Throughout the evening she had felt his nearness and his strength and his deep understanding, helping Agatha, helping Edwina, helping them all through an occasion which could have been a disastrous failure. As it was, his wit and vitality had buoyed their flagging conversation. He and Phillip between them had carried the evening to an amiable, if not a successful, conclusion.

She said impulsively: 'Charles—thank you for what you did on Saturday evening.'

He looked at her in surprise. It was the first time she had used his Christian name voluntarily, and his delight was immeasurable.

'You were wonderful,' she continued. 'Understanding and helpful.'

'Nonsense! I did nothing.'

She shook her head at him.

'Was it nothing to tide everyone through an embarrassing situation? A painful one for that poor woman. I wonder why Michael did such a thing?'

'Phillip was telling me his story, briefly, when we were alone. I feel sorry for the boy.'

'So do I, but I feel sorry for his mother, too. So does Agatha. I'm sure that was why she invited her—hoping to bring them together again.'

'Agatha Trent is a dear—but impulsive. Perhaps that is why she is a dear! She might have been wiser to confide in her brother beforehand and plan some other way, some other meeting. Still—it's easy to be wise after the event, isn't it?' He smiled, and she observed the laughter lines which were etched about his mouth, like brackets. He continued gently: 'That sweet sister of yours took Mrs. Shearing under her wing most valiantly, considering . . .'

'Considering what?'
'That she might have antagonized Michael forever in doing so. And I suspect that Michael means a lot to Charity.'
'You mean she loves him?'
'I think so. Don't you?'
'I've wondered . . . Oh, Charles, if Charity is in love it will go very deep with her.'
'That is love, Faith.'
She was surprised by the intense seriousness of his voice. She had not imagined that he could be like this. Suspecting her thoughts, he smiled ruefully.
'I'm not *all* light-hearted banter, my dear. Does that surprise you? Do you still consider me irresponsible?'
'No—' she answered slowly. 'Not any more . . .'
How could she, after that evening? His strength had fortified and comforted. On the journey home she had felt his nearness and his integrity, like a warm protective cloak. The memory of it had remained with her throughout yesterday.
He said quietly, seriously: 'I'm glad of that, Faith. So very glad . . .'
In the quietness of the laboratory, they looked at one another, and something exquisite and tender hovered between them, something which seemed suspended, crystal clear, from heaven itself. Something so delicate and fragile that a breath could

shatter it . . .

And into the moment cut the sharp sound of an opening door.

It was Doctor Stacey. His bland face was creased with concern.

'Have you seen Doctor Shearing?' he asked abruptly. 'I thought he might be here—'

'He hasn't dropped in this morning,' Faith told him, then, arrested by his expression, added: 'Do you want him urgently?'

'Not I. But the super. does.'

A summons by the medical superintendent did not always mean trouble, but, judging by Stacey's face, it augured that way now.

'Anything wrong?' Charles asked. His resentment at the man's abrupt intrusion began to fade.

The senior physician gave a resigned shrug.

'I'm afraid so. Over the Ransom girl. Her mother has written direct to the superintendent complaining about him.'

'What a detestable thing to do!' Faith protested hotly.

'On what grounds?' Charles asked.

'She's got some bee in her bonnet about her daughter's premature discharge.'

'Or the girl has,' Charles said wryly. 'If she is anything like that sister of hers, I wouldn't trust her an inch.'

Doctor Stacey said stiffly: 'If you are referring to Mrs. Drake, I think her particularly charming.'

'Oh, she's charming, all right,' Charles retorted. 'Some people think even snakes are.'

Faith spluttered. Nevertheless, she thought, the comparison was not inapt. Felicity's silken voice had warned Michael on Saturday evening—warned him with the purring delight of a cat. 'Watch out for my mother,' she had said: 'she's after your blood . . .' Or words to that effect.

'I don't imagine Doctor Shearing will be cowed by an unjustified complaint, Stacey. Why should he be? From all accounts the Ransom girl could have gone home days ago.'

'That's as may be,' Stacey muttered. 'All the same—' He turned toward the door.

'If he looks in, I'll tell him,' Faith offered, and Charles's voice added: 'Couldn't you do something yourself? Explain to the super. all the circumstances? The man's human. He'll understand. And he's sufficiently experienced, I imagine, to have met troublesome parents before . . .'

Stacey shrugged again, and departed. Uneasiness nagged at him like a guilty conscience. Temerity vied with a desire to protect his young assistant. All the same, he argued, the fellow had been a bit high-handed ever since he came, throwing his weight about and speaking his mind in a way that was decidedly tactless. And Doctor Stacey was all for tact. Peace at any price, was his motto. Please everyone and you can't go wrong. He quite overlooked the fact that in endeavoring to antagonize no one he failed to succeed in pleasing anyone. He steered a negative course always, and thought it safe.

If there was going to be trouble, he resolved to keep out of it. He had done his best to soothe the fractious Miss Ransom, so could not be blamed if his hot-headed young assistant did otherwise. He wondered anxiously whether the backwash of any row—if there was going to be a row—would overflow and envelop himself. Devoutly, he prayed not. He had a comfortable, safe post at this hospital and wanted it to stay that way.

He was returning from the pathological laboratory when the staff nurse from Matthew's ward came hurrying toward him. 'Oh, there you are, Doctor!' she said anxiously. 'Sister sent me to find you. It's the patient in bed number seven—the one with heart disease—'

He said sharply: 'Well, what is it?'

'Would you come to her at once, Sister says? There's a new swelling, sir—'

He hurried down to the ward, forgetful of young Doctor Shearing and the superintendent. Alarm rose like an engulfing tide. He felt apprehensive and afraid. The feeling had been increasing of late, whenever he thought of the patient in Matthew's ward. Everything pointed to heart disease. Every symptom was there. And yet she did not yield to treatment.

Of course, he argued to reassure himself, the pneumonia which preceded it had been bad. The woman had little resistance. It would take time. She had to gather strength. He thought of a hundred reasons and excuses. He was adept at excuses, adept at sidestepping issues; afraid of anything going wrong.

And yet a voice echoed in his memory—the voice of young Doctor Shearing saying: *'I wondered, sir—about her lymphatic glands . . .'*

And Doctor Willstack, too. *'I presume her lymphatic glands have been checked up on?'*

But what did *he* know about diagnosis? He was a pathologist. Microbes were his job; guinea-pigs his patients. These pathologists were always looking for trouble; always looking for the obscure, the unlikely, the remote possibility. Contemptuously, Doctor Stacey dismissed him. *And* that young assistant, too—his mind full of theories backed by no practical experience. The best thing he could do was to ignore the pair of them and stand by his own judgment.

But he couldn't stand by it when he saw the patient. And the damnable part of it was that young Shearing was there, beside her bed, with Sister Matthew frowning and looking anxious, disturbed out of her usual impassivity. They stepped aside, both of them, when he appeared. The staff nurse brought screens and erected them. Doctor Stacey rapped: 'All right,

Shearing—you can leave this to me.' The truth was that he didn't want his assistant around if by any ghastly chance he had really made a mistaken diagnosis.

Michael left the ward. It wasn't until later—much later—that a harassed senior physician remembered his message from the superintendent, and by that time he had other things, more serious things, to worry about; things which made the Ransom affair seem paltry and unimportant.

Walking down the corridor outside, Michael thought: I must see Charity. Now, right away. In the midst of his anxiety the thought of her was like a gentle hand laid upon his brow. He wondered whether he could confide his true fears about that woman in bed number seven and decided that perhaps it would be wiser, as yet, to discuss it with no one. Because if his suspicion was correct, his senior physician wouldn't want the situation discussed at all. And that, thought Michael sympathetically, would be quite understandable.

CHAPTER SIXTEEN

Charity was alone in the physiotherapy quarters when Michael sought her. That was lucky, he thought. If she'd had a patient they would have been unable to talk.

She was obviously clearing up after the last patient and preparing for the next, spreading the treatment couch with fresh linen. He watched her sensitive hands for a moment, delighting in their movements, but it wasn't long before she detected his presence.

'The door was open,' he said, 'so I just walked in. Do you mind?'

'Of course not. Why should I?'

He hesitated.

'I thought perhaps, after Saturday night, you might not wish to see me.'

She turned and faced him. Her voice was very gentle—so, too, was her smile.

'Of course I wish to see you, Michael.'

'I'd like to explain—if I can.'

'You don't have to, you know. I think perhaps I understand. I hope I understand.'

'No one can understand,' he said. 'I'm not sure that I do myself.'

Her heart was wrenched with pity for him, but because she knew that pity would be hateful to him, she hid it. Quietly, she waited. Her heart trembled because of his nearness. The fact that he had deliberately sought her out made her deeply happy, but this, also, she hid.

At last he spoke. 'I turned my back upon my mother,' he said slowly.

'I know.'

The old defiance returned to his voice.

'I suppose that seems a terrible thing

to you?'

'It seems an unhappy thing, Michael.'

'Don't be tolerant and patient and understanding with me!' he cried.

She was silent, stung by his anger. How could she ever get near him; how could she ever break through his pain? For it was pain—she knew that now. Bitterness was the soreness of it, the festering, the bleeding. She wanted, more than anything, to assuage and comfort, but he would have none of it.

'I suppose you know the story?' he asked abruptly.

'Snatches, probably quite inaccurate and unjustified.'

'What makes you think that?'

'Gossip is always inaccurate.'

'I wish I could believe that,' he said quietly.

'It stands to reason, if you are willing to listen to reason.'

'Don't lecture me—please.'

Charity took a deep breath.

'It's a pity,' she said, 'that someone didn't lecture you long ago.'

How much effort it cost her to speak to him thus, to suppress her strong desire to take him in her arms and comfort him, he would never know.

'What do you mean?' he asked.

'Simply that you have been feeling sorry for yourself far too long.'

'Sorry for myself!'

'Haven't you?' she asked calmly. 'Haven't you always thought of yourself as the boy whose mother deserted him? Perhaps your father has done the same—visualized himself as the wronged husband.' She felt his rising anger and continued resolutely. 'I don't expect you to like hearing this. And you don't have to listen if you don't want to. You can go right now, if you wish.'

He had no idea how terrified she was lest he do so. Once he turned his back and walked out of that door, she would have lost him—she knew that. Yet instinct urged her to challenge him, to upbraid him, to rouse his indignation. She did not really think him guilty of self-pity. His trouble always had been too much loneliness and too much introspection, but if she could jerk him away from grief, so much the better. She might then goad him to some action designed to prove his lack of self-pity—and that would lead him in only one direction.

'Go on—' he said grimly.

'There's nothing more to say, really.'

'Except that my behavior on Saturday was inexcusable.'

'I didn't say that,' she answered carefully.

'But you thought it.'

'Not now. At the time, perhaps. But I've had time in which to think since then. And perhaps you have, too.'

So she wasn't condemning him completely—that was something, he reflected.

He walked about the room, saying nothing. She went on with her work. Suddenly he spoke.

'How long have you known my mother? You do know her, don't you?'

'Yes, I've known her for a few months. We got to know each other quite well during our brief conversations in the café. But we never exchanged names. It seemed unnecessary.'

'So you didn't know her identity?'

'Of course not. It would have meant nothing to me, anyway, before you came to the hospital. She's been at the café throughout the summer season.'

'All that time!' There was something piteous in his voice, and Charity smiled at him gently.

'Believe me, Michael, she likes it. You don't have to feel sorry for her.'

'I'm not sorry for her!' he cried.

But he was, and she knew it. He knew it, too. And there was more than pity in his heart. There was self-reproach. A son should not let his mother work, if he could possibly help her.

'She likes the work,' Charity told him gently. 'She finds it interesting, and she does it well. How well, I can vouch.'

'That's beside the point,' Michael said gruffly, and she knew, with a quickening of her heart, that he hated the idea of his mother working for her living. He continued abruptly: 'That woman who helps her, the slovenly creature in the kitchen—'

'Yes, Michael?'

'She called my mother by the name of Shearing—'

'Naturally.'

'But she married again!'

'But she didn't, Michael.' Charity turned, came toward him, stood in front of him. Her sightless eyes seemed to look right into his heart. 'Agatha Trent knows the true story. You could get it from her. Better still, you could hear it from your mother, if you really want to.'

He made one last clutch at his old defiance. 'What makes you think I do?'

'Because you are a human being with a heart, Michael, whether you are willing to admit it, or not. And so is she. No human being should condemn another without at least giving him a chance of a hearing. You owe your mother that, Michael. *You owe it to her.*'

He answered quietly: 'What makes you think I haven't already thought of that?' He turned and left the room.

Nurse Warren was coming out of Caroline Ransom's private ward as Michael passed. Through the open door Caroline saw him. Her innocent baby-blue eyes missed nothing. She called swiftly: 'Good morning, Doctor Shearing!'

Michael paused. Bunny Warren held the door open for him. There was nothing else to do but enter.

Caroline was sitting in an armchair beside her window. She couldn't see much outside, he reflected, through the mass of flowers decorating the sill. The place was like a miniature Kew Gardens, he thought. A detached part of his mind observed that the color of her dressing gown—an elaborate satin affair—matched the pinky-mauve chrysanthemums banked around her.

She waited until Nurse Warren had closed the door, then turned a glance upon him which was both appealing and reproachful.

'You haven't been to see me for days, Doctor.'

'A slight exaggeration, Miss Ransom. I saw you a few days ago, when I pronounced you well enough to go home.'

'I *wish* you wouldn't call me Miss Ransom! And I don't feel well enough to go home!'

'You will, as soon as you get out of this hothouse atmosphere. All you need is a break from too much nursing—a patient *can* have too much nursing. It is up to you now. You've got to get out of here, get home, and get cracking.'

'But I can't even walk!'

'Of course not. You're not getting enough exercise. Stand up.'

She stared at him, her wide blue eyes bewildered and frightened. He snapped: 'Come on—get up!'

Valiantly she clutched the sides of her chair.

Valiantly she strove to rise, whimpered, and fell back helplessly.'

'Stand up,' he commanded quietly.

'I can't! I can't!'

He took hold of her wrists and gently but firmly pulled her to her feet. She clung to him, then, trembling. He felt her slender fingers holding onto him with surprising strength. 'You're so strong!' she whispered. 'So big and strong!'

He wanted to shake her. Instead, he released her hands, stepped aside, and said: 'Now walk.'

She whimpered again. She was enjoying herself vastly, and he knew it. She was as transparent as a pane of glass, and as empty.

She took a faltering step, and fell back into her chair, sobbing.

'I can't! *I can't!*'

He stood over her.

'Shall I tell you why you can't, Miss Ransom? Because you don't want to.'

'It isn't true!' She looked up at him with helpless appeal, and before he knew what was happening her arms were about his neck, clinging to him. 'I can, if you help me!' she sobbed. 'You're so big and strong, Doctor!'

He felt a moment of panic. Such women were dangerous. Doctors had been caught by them before, and compromised to their professional detriment. He thought: No calculating little schemer like this is going to make a hash of *my* career! and he took hold of her wrists roughly, forcing them apart. For all their slenderness, they had the strength of a vice, pinioning him about the neck. He could feel their grip upon the back of his collar. She laughed softly, her face very near his own, her mouth sensuous and inviting. She said: 'I can see myself reflected in your eyes, Doctor—nice eyes, all dark and suggestive! They must break an awful lot of hearts!' Her voice was low and husky now, and he felt a question detach itself from the confusion of his mind. How often had she practised it? What film star did she get this voice from? But far from attracting him, it repelled.

Everything about her was repellent: her insincerity, her artifice, her guile. She had too much make-up on her face and too much perfume about her person.

'How old are you?' he asked abruptly, looking at her as if she were some organic specimen in which he had nothing but a scientific interest.

'Eighteen.'

Eighteen! Heaven knows what she'll be like at twenty-eight! he thought disgustedly, and with an agile twist which caught her completely off her guard, jerked away from her. He was free of her determined grasp.

She was so astonished that for a moment she forgot even to whimper. Then she remembered her act and continued with it, renewing her helpless appeal, rubbing her wrists and saying with reproach: 'Doctor—you *hurt* me!'

'Not nearly so much as I could with a slipper,' he said brutally.

She chose to treat that as a joke, giving a high-pitched little titter which she believed to be childlike and adorable. To Michael it was merely irritating.

'You're joking!' she protested.

He decided to end the conversation. He turned toward the door, saying with professional impatience: 'If you want to walk, you *can* walk. If you don't, you'll be nothing but a nuisance to everyone. Practise a few steps daily, then a few more and a few more. Once you get home you'll find your desire to walk increasing, because otherwise you'll be bored. It isn't wise to linger in a hospital once you are fit enough to leave. It has a bad psychological effect. You begin to imagine that you'll never get well and to accept the habit of being nursed. Get away from all that, and you'll forge ahead. Nursing is only valuable so long as it is essential. After that it is up to the patient.'

He had reached the door. His hand was upon the knob. Her baby-blue eyes were no longer wide and helpless and appealing; they were narrowed in anger. She wanted to hit back, to punish him for his indifference. She said softly:

'My sister came to see me yesterday afternoon.'

'Indeed?'

The knob was turning.

'She told me about Saturday night.'

The knob was still.

'What about Saturday night?' he asked levelly.

'You were at the same dinner party, I believe.'

'Well?'

'But you didn't stay . . .'

He shut the door. He came back and stood before her. She felt a momentary shiver of fear. Had she gone too far? If so, it was too late to turn back. She clutched at resentment and decided to punish him thoroughly. No man should be allowed to reject her so summarily.

'Go on,' he said. 'Say what you want to say.'

Her glance was limpid and trusting, affecting an innocence quite out of character. This girl wasn't innocent when she was born, he thought cynically.

She opened her eyes wide.

'Why, I do believe you are angry!' she reproached him.

'Why should I be?'

'No reason that I can think of! I was going to sympathize, that was all. No matter what other people might say, *I* understand.'

'About what?' he asked abruptly.

Really, she thought, his voice was too stirring for words. Crisp and deep, even when he rapped out a question like that. Anger in a man could be rather fascinating, she discovered, reveling in the brute force of him.

'About the way you behaved,' she answered. 'I don't blame you for it. I'd walk out on *my* mother if she were an adulteress.'

She was terrified by his reaction. For the first time in her selfish little life she was really afraid. His face darkened with anger so intense that she shrank from it.

She had gone too far; said too much. She realized that now. But her desire to punish him had goaded and goaded. All along she had wanted to hit out at him, to make him aware of her—somehow, anyhow. Well, she had succeeded. He had noticed her at last —but not in the way she wished.

He wanted to strike her. She knew it with a swift and unerring instinct. He wanted to strike her down, to wipe out the memory of her words.

Instead, he was terrifyingly calm. His only physical reaction was the sudden clenching of his hands at his sides, and a pulse beating swiftly in his temple. He said quietly: 'No one uses that word in connection with my mother—understand? No one—*no one, Miss Ransom*—gives her that name. Not to me—or behind my back, if they are wise.'

She burst out defiantly: 'Why not? She can't

mean anything to you, surely? Why, the whole of Highcliffe knows her story; everyone has heard it! Your father divorced her because she was no good!'

'My father,' he said, 'made a mistake. I know that now. But I won't let anyone condemn either of them—understand? Everyone, at some time in his life, makes a mistake of some kind. You made one just now—a bad one, Miss Ransom. And one I shall never forget or forgive.'

She cried shrilly: '*You* should talk about mistakes! What about your own?'

'I am as capable of mistakes as the next person—but not deliberate ones, I hope, like yours.'

'Oh, no!' she mocked. 'You're the sort of doctor who makes the mistake of ill-treating your patients, driving them out of bed before they are fit to get up, and out of hospital before they are ready to leave! But you'll regret it, mark my words!'

'What you are trying to say,' he answered indifferently, 'is that I shall regret not succumbing to your determined little schemes. That I shall regret I did not flatter you, and respond to you; regret not falling for you. My dear girl, what you don't realize is that every doctor at some time or another is unfortunate enough to get a patient like you. Every doctor is acquainted with the cheap little flirt who thinks she can enjoy herself with him. When you are older you'll become the type of woman who deliberately sets out to compromise her doctor.' He finished in a burst of anger: 'What sort of a fool do you take me for? The sooner you get out of this hospital, the better. You could have gone home days ago, but you were enjoying yourself too much.'

He turned upon his heel, but before he reached the door again she flung at him:

'Don't worry—I'm going. But so are you! You didn't know that, did you? Well, you know now. Mother has written to the medical superintendent complaining about your treatment of me, and a good thing, too. You'll be sorry you weren't nicer to me, Doctor Shearing!'

'Sorry?' he echoed. 'I'm only sorry that I kept my patience so long! Your mother can do her darnedest, as far as I am concerned.'

There was a tap upon the door. It opened to admit little Nurse Warren.

'Doctor Shearing—the superintendent's secretary has been telephoning all over the hospital for you—'

'I think I know what for. He wants to see me in his office,' Michael said. 'Thank you, Nurse. I'll go right away.'

All agog, Nurse Warren departed—back to the ward kitchen, back to the excited speculation of the nurses. Rumors were already flying about the hospital as to why the super. wanted to see young Doctor Shearing.

There seemed only one possible explanation, although Staff Nurse Connell wouldn't allow any of them to voice it. She liked Doctor Shearing, she told them indignantly, and dared any one of them to say a word against him. But then, Hope Connell was like that. All the Connell sisters were like that: loyal and friendly, liking the whole world.

And really, there *was* something likable about Doctor Shearing, despite his taciturn manner. The patients loved him. But he never noticed any of the nurses. Just aprons and starched uniforms—that's all we are to that young man! Bunny thought ruefully. It was really very disappointing. None of the new men had proved at all susceptible, so far—although the lab. boy *did* say that Doctor Willstack's roving eye roved just as far as his assistant—and no farther.

Behind the closed door of Caroline Ransom's private ward Doctor Shearing met his patient's challenging and malicious eyes. Well, Doctor, they said, what did I tell you? This is it!

He smiled unexpectedly, provoking her with his laughter. Her eyes narrowed in anger. He bowed mockingly and said: 'Good morning, Miss Ransom!' and departed.

CHAPTER SEVENTEEN

Phillip Trent entered Matthew's ward just as Doctor Stacey was leaving bed number seven. Something about the physician arrested his attention. The man looked tense and worried, and Sister Matthew, behind his back, regarded him with stern disapproval.

Something had gone wrong—that was obvious.

Doctor Stacey walked down the ward unseeingly. Phillip waited for him by the door.

'Anything wrong?' he asked in a low voice. He didn't want that martinet of a Sister to hear.

Stacey blinked and looked at him, as if from a distance. Then he jerked back to reality with a start. He was about to speak when he saw Sister and Staff Nurse coming toward him, so he remained silent, waiting for them to go.

But Sister Matthew paused, looked at Phillip respectfully, and said: 'You've come to see the hernia, sir?'

'How is she?'

'Splendid, sir. It really is amazing how swiftly hernias recover, after excruciating pain. A few days, and all is well. *Your* patient is no exception, sir.'

She spoke with almost exaggerated affability, with an air of innuendo which did not escape Phillip and most certainly did not escape Doctor Stacey. She was taking a dig at him, and he knew it. Before long the entire nursing staff would be gossiping and whispering—he knew that, too. Over in the nurses' home the story would spread like a bush fire. The ward kitchens would hum with it. Sister Matthew would tell her bosom friend Sister Luke—'Nosy Parker,' the nurses called her, he thought not inaptly. He could imagine these two cronies pecking over it like a pair of crows over a tid-bit. He suddenly hated the lot of them—all affability toward the medicals so long as a case went smoothly; blaming them behind their backs, if not.

But anyone could make a mistake, he thought wretchedly. Doctors weren't oracles. It was the first serious mistake he had made in all his years at St. Bede's—but that would not be accepted as an excuse, of course.

He paused irresolutely. He badly wanted to talk to someone, to confide in someone, and Phillip Trent was sane and unbiased and fair-minded and experienced. He'd understand—surely he would understand! And even if he didn't, he might offer some sound advice as to what to do in the circumstances.

All the same, in his heart Stacey knew what he had to do. Take the rap.

He felt sick at the thought, sick over his own blundering and stupidity. He could blame no one but himself. Even young Doctor Shearing had suspected, the first time he saw the case. Doctor Willstack, too. That perhaps was the most galling part of the whole business—that newcomers should see what he had overlooked. That his own junior should think of something which had not even crossed his mind.

He wished now that he had followed Shearing's suggestion at the time, but so sure had he been of his own judgment, so convinced that the young doctor was barking up the wrong tree, that he had rejected the idea.

Phillip got away from Sister Matthew as soon as he could.

As soon as they were out of earshot he said: 'Do you want to tell me about it?'

'I must tell someone or go mad,' Stacey said. 'That patient of mine was supposed to be suffering from heart disease. I diagnosed it myself. All the symptoms were there, so I treated it accordingly.'

'But it didn't yield?' Phillip asked.

'Not a scrap. We persisted, but it made no difference. Now I know why. It isn't heart at all, but a malignancy of the lymphatic glands—between a cancerous and a benign condition.'

'Hodgkin's disease?'

The senior physician nodded briefly. He looked wretched—and no wonder, thought Phillip, feeling suddenly sorry for the man.

'Look here,' he said comfortingly, 'don't

blame yourself too much. It's a common error, you know. The symptoms are often indistinguishable in the early stages. Shortness of breath, irregular heart action, and so forth. The most experienced diagnosticians have been known to confuse the two.'

'All the same, I should have checked up—especially when it was suggested to me.'

'By whom?' asked Phillip quickly.

'Believe it or not, by my own assistant.'

'Young Shearing!'

'He first. Then Willstack.'

Phillip was silent a moment. Mingled with his sympathy for the physician was an inevitable criticism. He felt proud of Michael and said thoughtfully: 'He's promising, is Michael Shearing.'

'He must be,' said Stacey glumly.

Phillip looked at him swiftly. He hoped the man would give his junior the credit he deserved, but he had a sneaking feeling that Stacey rather resented him. It would be an effort for him to praise Michael, especially to the hospital authorities. He asked swiftly: 'What are you going to do?'

'What can I do?'

'Go straight to the super. and tell him. What else?'

What else, indeed? Stacey saw all his security, all his peace of mind, all the untroubled comfort which he had built about himself go whistling down the wind. Was it so flimsy, then, that the first breath of disaster could shatter it? If so, had it been worth all the struggle, all the careful side-stepping, all the evasions and tact and careful amiability which he had nurtured throughout the years? That, he had thought, was the way to keep his job. The line of least resistance, always. Agree with everyone, and please everyone. Not for him the forthright attitude of young Doctor Shearing. Not for him the outspokenness which made enemies. Play for safety—that had been his creed.

And where had it gotten him? Precisely nowhere when trouble came along. There'd be no side-stepping *this* issue. And out of all the people he had been so careful to pander to, who would stick up for him? He couldn't think of one.

'I've got to get down to Luke's,' Phillip said when they reached the staff elevator. He looked at Stacey's wretched face and felt irritated, as well as pitying. Then suddenly he smiled.

'If it's any comfort to you,' he said, 'you're not the first doctor to have made a wrong diagnosis.'

'But I've always been so careful!'

Careful of what? Phillip wondered. Careful not to tread on people's toes, not to ruffle them, not to antagonize or upset them? He knew that Doctor Stacey would never have shown the forthright courage of Doctor

Shearing in telling the Ransom girl, for instance, that she was fit enough to go home. Oh dear me, no! thought Phillip, grimly. He'd stroke Lady Ransom's sables for her until she purred.

But even beneath his contempt, he felt pity for the man. He wondered how he would come out of this—courageous, or cowed?

He said unexpectedly: 'You have a chance now to prove yourself, Stacey,' and stepped into the staff elevator. He had closed the door and sailed downward before the senior physician had time to ask what he meant.

Glumly, Doctor Stacey proceeded on his way. He wasn't quite sure where he was going. He paced the hospital corridors unseeingly, avoiding the elevator, descending staircase after staircase until he reached the ground floor. In all the hospital there was no place in which he could be alone. His room, over in the resident's quarters, would be given over to domestic hands. The staff room would be occupied by someone: it always was. There was nowhere else.

He took a deep breath. What was the use, anyway, of hiding, thinking, brooding? Better face the music and get it over. There was no other way. Perhaps it was better to make a clean breast of his mistake than to wait for it to be found out, to allow rumor and gossip to spread their poison. The thought awakened an unfamiliar decisiveness within him, and at once he felt unaccountably better, like a man who decides to have a troublesome tooth extracted.

He turned toward the passage leading to the medical superintendent's office. It was concealed by swinging doors and paneled in sombre mahogany. It struck a chill into his heart. He felt as if he were approaching the condemned cell.

The door of the superintendent's office opened, and Michael came out. Doctor Stacey stood still abruptly, remembering that some time ago—and what ages it now seemed!—he had been looking for Doctor Shearing, to tell him to report to the super's office. He had forgotten all about that. Now the whole thing seemed trivial and the Ransom girl no more than a troublesome fly, to be brushed away. For the first time in his life Stacey forgot his own trouble in the face of another's. He said abruptly: 'I hope it wasn't too bad, Shearing? I mean—I hope the super. didn't take too harsh a view? If it will help, I'll support your dismissal of the Ransom girl. I should have done that, anyway. Maybe it isn't too late.'

Michael looked at him in surprise.

'That's all right—' he said uncomfortably. 'We have to learn, I suppose, not to throw our weight about too much.'

'Why shouldn't we?' Stacey demanded with surprising aggression. 'I've come to the conclusion, Shearing, that it isn't always wise to play a safe game. It's what I've always done, and now I regret it. One little flick, and your house of cards comes tumbling down . . .'

Michael's steady eyes looked at him with sudden interest.

'Is anything wrong?' he asked.

Stacey's rather prim mouth tilted wryly.

'Everything, Shearing. You were right about that heart patient, number seven in Matthew. And I was wrong. That's all.'

'You mean—'

'I mean that your observation about her lymphatic glands was sound. Need I say more?'

A deep concern spread over Michael's face. He put out his hand with spontaneous sympathy and touched the older man's white sleeve.

'I'm sorry,' he said awkwardly.

'You ought to be glad. You proved your worth rather early in your career. I've undermined my own. That's all.' He gave an unexpected grin and turned toward the super's office. Michael spoke to him as he tapped upon the door, but the senior physician did not seem to hear. All he heard was the brief summons from within. It sounded like the voice of Doom, passing sentence upon him.

Michael lingered a moment, feeling shocked and concerned. The senior physician's news drove all thought of his own interview out of his head. And it hadn't been too bad, anyway. The medical superintendent had been surprisingly human. 'It isn't always wise,' he said reasonably, 'to be too aggressive in our dealings with patients. No matter how trying they are, remember there is always someone waiting to catch us, always someone willing to accuse a doctor of negligence or incompetence—or worse. St. Bede's has never yet had a defamatory charge laid against it.'

'Nor can it now, sir! The girl is well enough to be sent home!' The wise, experienced eyes had smiled into his own.

'I know that. It might surprise you to know that I have my finger on the hospital pulse. A superintendent's job isn't executed entirely from behind a desk.' He tapped the accusing letter with the back of his hand. 'This sort of thing frequently emanates from the relatives of our most troublesome and least ailing patients. The thing to learn, Shearing, is how to avoid them.'

'But I can't kowtow and back-scratch and hand out false sympathy, sir!'

'It isn't a matter of being servile, my boy. It is a matter of being firm without bludgeoning—or without giving anyone the excuse to accuse you of bludgeoning. I consider you were right in sticking to your guns—but don't go blowing them off until the enemy refuses, point-blank, to retreat.' The keen eyes smiled again. Michael felt the liking behind them, and was surprised by it. When he came to St. Bede's he had expected no one to like him.

Now he found that it meant quite a lot to him to have the approval of his medical superintendent.

'I'll deal with this letter, Doctor. I have dealt with them before. It isn't a job I enjoy, so I hope you'll spare me the trouble of receiving them in future. I shall uphold your action, of course, even if Lady Ransom chooses to go higher—but somehow, when she has my answer, I don't think she will . . .'

And surprisingly, unexpectedly, he had held out his hand. His grip had been firm and encouraging. Although Michael did not know it, the medical superintendent of St. Bede's was going to enjoy taking Lady Ransom down a peg or two, and the junior physician's courage had earned his respect, not his condemnation.

All the same, as he left the holy of holies Michael's hot-headedness had learned its first, and unforgettable lesson. He was learning a lot of things lately, he mused as he went on his way. He was even learning to like the world and the people who inhabited it. He was discovering that he had a heart.

And it was Charity who had introduced him to it.

CHAPTER EIGHTEEN

During visiting hours the entire staff breathed a sigh of relief and relaxed. In the ward kitchen the nurses grabbed a welcome cup of tea, gulping it down as they cut bread and butter, set trays and tea trolleys, and prepared for the tea-hour rush. The atmosphere even penetrated the pathological laboratory, where Tommy, the lab. boy, whistled as he put on the kettle and the pathologist and his assistant paused briefly in their labors.

Tommy enjoyed this hour—especially since the new Chief had come. It was like taking a deep breath of fresh air and slowly exhaling it. Miss Connell enjoyed it, too—he could tell. She was different, was Miss Connell, from the old days. Of course she'd always been nice to him, never spoke to him crossly or anything like that, but she had never seemed entirely human. All dignified, thought Tommy, as he slapped teaspoons into saucers and saved a bit of milk for the guinea-pigs in their cages. That was how she was, in old Doc Walker's day. Now she smiled a lot more, and chatted, and laughed at Doctor Willstack's jokes. And a rare one for jokes was Doctor Willstack.

That didn't mean he wasn't a worker, too. Work! Tommy told Nurse Warren, down in Luke's, expressively. He worked you all right—

and himself. But somehow you enjoyed it. There was a zest to it.

Tommy liked popping down to the ward kitchens. When Doctor Willstack sent him down with a blood count for Sister Parker, in Luke's, he went willingly. He liked teasing the nurses, and asking Bunny Warren what boy she was walking out with now, and dodging swiftly if Sister appeared. He liked to see what was going on down there, in the wards. In the scientific isolation of the laboratory, the hum of hospital life became remote and dimmed.

He liked roaming the corridors, too. One of the theatre orderlies was his uncle, and he didn't half have some juicy tales to tell. Juicy, said Nurse Warren, was an unfortunate word—but she knew what he meant. 'S'wonderful,' said Tommy, 'the things they do up there! Especially Mr. Trent. My uncle says he's a something-genius, the things he does to people and sends'm out whole again.'

Staff Nurse Connell heard him say that. Her face lit up with a sort of pride, and she answered, although he hadn't really been talking to her: 'I believe he *is* a genius. He *is* wonderful. Wonderful and humane. Look at old Mrs. Tompkins—almost ready to go home. And the patients love him . . .'

'*And* the nurses!' chanted Bunny Warren with a sigh. 'I've been head-over heels in love with him since the day he arrived! But of course he never notices the likes of me.' Her eyes twinkled and her glance turned suggestively to Hope Connell as she finished: 'Staff nurses are what *he* likes!'

Staff Nurse Connell ignored that, which was surprising, really, because she was always ready with a comeback. Took the nurses' teasing and gave plenty in return, she did. But not today. Today she turned away, hiding her face. Or she thought she was hiding it. She forgot the mirror on the wall which one of the nurses, defying authority, had dared to install. Her features, with their deep, betraying blush, were clearly revealed in it.

Tommy also liked visiting the physiotherapy quarters, because Nurse Connell's sister always had a tidbit of some kind for him. A bar of chocolate, or sweets. She bought them for the child patients, she said. Today he wandered up hopefully. He was flat broke and wouldn't have a penny until payday, and a few sweets, in the meantime, wouldn't come amiss.

But his luck was out. She was pressing the button for the staff elevator when he reached her corridor. He ran forward and held the gate open for her, and she rewarded him with her lovely smile.

'Going out, miss?' he asked cheerfully.

'Just for a breath of air, Tommy,' she answered, recognizing his voice.

He watched the departing elevator regretfully, then, whistling, turned back to the laboratory. Kettle should be boiling its lid off by now, and Doctor Willstack would have something to say about steam affecting the instruments. Guiltily, Tommy broke into a run. When he burst into the laboratory the chief pathologist and his assistant moved away from each other. They'd been talking. They did that a lot, lately. Tommy's sharp eyes surveyed them speculatively. First there was Nurse Connell, down in Luke's, blushing like anything because Nurse Warren teased her about Mr. Trent, and now her sister did the same, moving away from Doctor Willstack. And Doctor Willstack wasn't any less obvious, turning back to his work table and studying it so intently anyone would have thought he was pretending to work . . .

And neither of them had noticed that the kettle was boiling its lid off . . .

Blandly, Tommy made the tea. He carried a cup across to Miss Connell's table.

'Going to the dance tomorrow night, miss?' he asked cheerfully.

'Yes, Tommy. I am.'

'I bet you'll look smashing, miss—if I may say so!' he added hastily.

'You may say so, Tommy, with the greatest of pleasure!' she answered gaily.

Gosh—she certainly *had* changed! In the old days he wouldn't have dared to pass a remark like that to her; she'd have frozen him with a glance.

The sound of a dog's shrill, ecstatic bark

echoed up from the courtyard below. Faith looked out with a smile. Mustard, waiting for Charity, barked his welcome. She watched her sister stoop, take hold of the leash, and walk with him across the courtyard, through the main gates, turning in the direction of the park.

* * *

The children were there again. Charity heard them as she approached. Snatches of their laughter came to her as she reached the top of the main drive and turned toward the wide reaches of the lake. They saw her approach, and came running.

'May Mustard play with us today? You did promise!'

'As soon as he delivers me safely to the café,' she smiled.

'Your friend is inside,' said the more precocious of the two children.

'My friend?' she asked, wondering if they meant Agatha or Edwina.

'The gentleman. The one who looks for you here.'

Charity's heart skipped a beat. The gentleman could be none other than Michael.

'When did he come?' she asked quietly.

'A few minutes ago,' said one.

'No—*ages* ago!' protested the other.

'Well, anyway, he was looking for Mustard,

the way he does. I could tell. Then he asked us if we had seen you. We said no, you hadn't come yet. So he went inside.'

Something compelled Charity to linger. If Michael had gone into the café, it might not have been in search of herself. She decided to wait awhile before intruding. If his mission was what she hoped, the scene was not one in which she should take part. It was between himself and his mother, no one else.

Quietly she sat down beside the lake. 'I'm not ready for my tea,' she told the children, 'but play with Mustard if you want to. And take care of him, won't you?'

'We will! We will!'

Charity stooped and released the dog's collar. He licked her hand in a frenzy of love and gratitude and raced away. She heard his barks mingled with the shrill cries of the children. The noise they made drowned the cry of gulls flying inland and the lapping of the water upon the shore. Perhaps it was this, coupled with the high screen of the rhododendron bushes, which deadened the sound of an engine, advancing up the drive. Whatever the reason, neither the children heard it, nor Charity.

Nor Mustard, racing after the ball they threw for him. It hit a tuft of grass and bounded off unexpectedly onto the road—straight beneath the wheels of a delivery van which rounded the corner at that moment.

The shriek of its brakes vied with the terrified yelping of an animal in pain.

One of the children screamed. Another sobbed. There was a flurry of flying feet, and still the frenzied yelping of the dog. Men's voices. And a woman's. *'Peter, you didn't ought to throw your ball about like that! I've told you before. Killed the pore animal, that's what you've done!'*

And above them all, Charity's voice calling with a mounting terror: 'Mustard! *Mustard—where are you?'*

Blindly, she stumbled forward in search of him.

* * *

When Michael reached the park, he looked around instinctively for Charity. He was not really surprised that she had not arrived, for he had come early—and deliberately, for he wanted to be there first. There was something he wanted to do before she came.

He walked up the wooden steps of the café, his feet echoing hollowly upon the boards. He opened the door and walked in, and the bell jangled shrilly in the little back room. He waited, and after a minute a woman came out.

She stood still abruptly, looking at him, waiting for him, perhaps, to turn his back upon her again. Instead, he took a step forward and said: 'I came to find you.'

'Why, Michael?'

Her voice was low and patient, with the patience of a woman who was accustomed to waiting.

'I wanted to talk to you.'

She made no answer, just waited again for him to speak. He said: 'I want to apologize—'

'For what?'

'Need you ask? For turning from you, as I did, at the Trents' the other night.'

'But I understood, Michael. I didn't blame you.'

'I blame myself.'

'Don't. There is no need.'

Silence again. Silence fraught with a poignant awareness and a need so deep and vast that it lay like a chasm between them.

He said awkwardly: 'Are you alone?'

'Yes. My kitchen help finished for the season last week-end.'

'Your kitchen help! I wonder if you realize how distasteful that sounds to me?'

'But why? To a woman who does a job like this, it sounds anything but distasteful.'

'Because I hate you *doing a* job like this!' he burst out angrily.

'There is no need. I like the work. I've done this sort of thing for many years, in different places. Unfortunately, I was equipped for nothing else.'

Michael said almost savagely: 'And he *let* you?'

'He?' she whispered.

'The man you left my father for,' he answered brutally.

The woman looked at him with an expression of pity and understanding. He felt ashamed and humbled by it. She did not hate him for his taunt, for his anger, for his tone of attack and accusation. She answered gently: 'I did not leave your father for any man.'

'But everyone knows you went away with Humphreys? My father knows it. I know it. The world knows it.'

'Then I must be the only person in the world who does not.'

They kept their distance, afraid to come closer to one another. She said quietly, with a firmness she had not possessed of old: 'I am telling you the truth, Michael. I'd like you to hear it—for the first time. It is up to you whether you believe it or not.'

To her astonishment, he answered: 'I don't want to hear it. All I want is to do what I set out to do.'

'And that?' she whispered.

'To bring you home.'

He saw her reel slightly, and steady herself against a chair. He moved toward her swiftly and took hold of her hands. They were roughened with work; quite unlike the smooth, indulged hands which had caressed him as a child.

'You don't mean that, Michael—'

'I do mean it. We want you there, my father and I.'

'Your father! I don't believe it. He told me—I remember so well—that he never wanted to see me again . . .'

'If you saw him now,' said Michael, 'I think you would pity him, as I do.'

'Would he pity me?' she smiled. 'I hope not. I wouldn't want him to feel as you do—ashamed because I am working here. That is your reason, perhaps, for wanting to take me home . . . and that is why I am refusing, Michael.'

He said urgently: 'Listen to me. I don't care what you did. The past is over and finished. You didn't marry Humphreys—I do know that, because Charity told me—'

The woman's face softened. 'Charity!' she said softly. 'Charity is the sweetest girl I have ever known, the most true and the most loyal . . .' She broke off and looked at him searchingly. 'Do you love her, Michael?' she asked abruptly.

'Yes, Mother. I do.'

Her tired face was lightened with happiness.

'I'm glad. Glad, Michael! Have you told her?'

'Of course not. I don't want to lose her friendship.'

'*Lose* her—my dear boy, what sort of an idea is this?'

'Simply that I know she doesn't love me in

return. How could she? How could any woman love a man like myself—ill-mannered, cynical, cruel—'

'You are none of those things at heart, Michael—I know that. I know the boy you were born, and fundamentally the heart doesn't change. I know that, too.' She shook her greying head at him gently. 'You say you don't want to hear the truth, Michael, but you shall. The truth is that I was once most wretchedly unhappy, and most wretchedly lonely. I loved your father, but I was awed by him, too. Awed by his seniority, and his pride, and his passion for rare and beautiful things. Sometimes he would go away for weeks at a stretch, searching for some treasure which he would bring home in triumph and gloat over for weeks. He forgot everyone at those moments—his wife, his son, his work, everything. He was a passionate collector.'

'Not any more,' Michael said. 'He hasn't bought a single treasure since the day you parted.'

Astonishment showed in her eyes. Then she said softly: 'Poor man—did he care so much about losing something which, in the end, proved worthless?'

'Meaning yourself?'

'I was never very comfortable upon the pedestal he placed me on,' Edwina said ruefully. 'I won't say more, nor excuse or condone my behavior. Tom Humphreys came along. He guessed a great many things I never told him. He comforted me—and I let him. There, I was weak. But it isn't always easy to be strong, Michael—'

'I know,' he said gently.

'But I didn't go away with him. I didn't love him, you see. I felt then that I didn't love anyone but you. But I lost you. All my protestations availed me nothing against Humphreys' damning admissions. I felt like a voice crying in the wilderness. I was lost.' She shrugged, turned away. 'There was nothing for me to do but stand upon my own two feet. I've stood upon them ever since. First in London, then wherever I could get work. A housekeeper down in Kent. A waitress in Winchester. Gradually, I worked my way back to Devon—'

'You never came to see me,' he said quietly.

'Whenever I tried, your father had taken you abroad. Legally, I was entitled to see you occasionally. Whenever those occasions arose, you had been whisked away somewhere. In the end I gave up. I thought it better. Better that you should put me out of your life altogether. But in my heart I always longed to return to Highcliffe—and in the end, I did.'

They were silent then. He found that he was still holding her hands. Suddenly his arms were around her. *'Come back, come back . . .'* he whispered. 'He needs you. We both need you . . . We *want you,* don't you understand?'

It was then that the sounds outside cut into the moment with disrupting finality. The grinding shriek of brakes; the cries of children; the piercing squeal of an animal in pain. And a girl's voice crying over and over again: *'Mustard! Mustard, where are you? Where are you?'*

Michael was out of the little wooden building in a flash. He saw Charity stumbling blindly upon the turf and in a moment he was beside her, his arms about her, holding her fast. Like a terrified bird, she was still.

'Darling—it's all right! Darling, you're safe! I've got you, and you're safe, my darling . . .'

'Michael! Oh, Michael!' She clung to him, her terror still a suffocating fog. He could feel her trembling, and his arms tightened protectively. She sobbed: *'Mustard! Find Mustard for me! He's hurt—killed! I heard someone say he was killed!'*

Gently, he lowered her into a park bench. Edwina was at her side, holding her, comforting her. He left them together and ran toward the accident. A group had gathered; Michael elbowed his way through. The driver of the van was on his knees beside Mustard's inert form.

'Let me see,' said Michael urgently. 'I'm not a vet, but I am a doctor.'

He lifted the animal's head gently. The agonized yelping had ceased and for a moment, seeing how still and lifeless he lay,

Michael feared the worst. Then, with relief, he felt the slow, unsteady beat of Mustard's heart.

'He's not dead!' he said swiftly. 'I think both his forelegs are broken—'

The driver of the van mopped his brow.

'I couldn't help it, sir—really I couldn't!' His face was white and upset. 'I've a dog myself,' he stammered. 'Wouldn't hurt a hair of its head . . .'

'I'm sure you wouldn't,' Michael murmured reassuringly, and, lifting Mustard gently from the ground, carried him into the little wooden building. Edwina followed with Charity.

'Have you a telephone here, Mother? I want to ring for a vet.'

Even at such a moment as this, he observed the happiness which leaped to Edwina's face when he called her by that name. She indicated the instrument swiftly, and Michael crossed to it, first laying Mustard gently upon the floor. 'He's all right, Charity—don't worry—he's all right.'

'Not killed?' she whispered. 'I heard someone screaming that he was killed!'

'A hysterical nursemaid, that's all.' He took her hand and led her toward the dog, and she went down upon her knees beside him, caressing his soft head with loving hands. When Michael returned from telephoning, she was still there upon the floor. He stooped and gathered her close to him. They did not speak. Edwina looked across the room and smiled.

She did not mind because, for the moment, they had forgotten her. Right now there was no one in their world but themselves. She felt a fountain of happiness leap within her heart because, at last, her son had found peace.

CHAPTER NINETEEN

St. Bede's Hospital held its annual staff ball at the beginning of the season, heralding winter activities with a blaze of color and music. The affair was held in the town hall—'red carpet, awning, and all the trimmings,' was how little Nurse Warren described it to the envious student nurse in Luke's, 'not forgetting, of course, our best party manners . . .'

'Oh, I *wish* I could go!' breathed the student nurse.

'Next year, ducky, you probably will. Invitations are by rota, you see. I've had to wait two years for mine!'

'What are you wearing? Something glamorous?'

'Glamorous—*me?*' Bunny gave her hearty laugh.

'I'm sure,' said the student nurse earnestly, 'that if you gave thought to your appearance, Nurse Warren, you could look quite charming.'

'Well, now, isn't that nice?' grinned Bunny.

'Cheek!' said the second-year nurse, who

was irritated by the student's patronage. Always out to air her knowledge, that girl was, or to impress her superiors. The girl talked like a medical dictionary, although it was doubtful if she understood all the terms. 'What makes you think *you're* so marvelous, anyway?'

'Oh, come off it, Taylor! Leave the kid alone,' urged Bunny good-naturedly.

'I'd have you know,' stated the student nurse, 'that I passed my exams with honors in three subjects.'

'Always the bright girl of the class, eh? Well, you're not back at school here, Miss Know-All, and your honors don't seem to have helped your bed-making! Nurse Connell walked into the ward this morning and saw those envelope corners of yours. She didn't say a word, because Sister was there, but she remade them. You're lucky to be under a decent staff nurse, take it from me!'

'I have the greatest respect for Nurse Connell,' the girl answered primly, 'but I would prefer to have my errors, if any, pointed out to me by her, rather than by you.'

'You wait until *I'm* a staff nurse, my girl. I'll be after your blood if you leave the open ends of pillow slips facing the door, *and* the castors turned outwards, which was what you did yesterday.'

'Oh, break it up, you two,' Bunny Warren urged. She never enjoyed these little dissensions which flared up in the ward kitchen occasionally. They spluttered like matches, and as quickly died. All the same, that student nurse *was* a little prig. Nurse Warren's good humor asserted itself rapidly. 'What do you think I should do,' she asked with a twinkle, 'to improve my unfortunate appearance?'

'Oh, I didn't *say* it was unfortunate!'

'You don't have to, my child. I weigh more in pounds than my height in inches. My mouth is too big and my nose too small. Glamorous! Me!' She laughed with genuine amusement.

'I should advise you to wear darker colors, in order to detract from your size. And a new hair style might help.'

Nurse Taylor cast her eyes ceilingwards. Another moment, she thought, and I'll hit that girl one.

'I suppose you realize,' she commented bitingly, 'that you are being impertinent, patronizing—*and* cruel? But no, you can't realize it—you simply can't, or you wouldn't do it. You just wouldn't *do* it!'

'Do what?' asked the student nurse, wide-eyed.

Nurse Taylor gave up. Bunny smiled good-naturedly.

'I've tried dozens of different hair-styles, but they make no difference, because my face remains the same!'

'And no one would want it to change!' declared Nurse Taylor. 'There isn't a person in this hospital, my dear little teacher's-pride-and-joy, who doesn't love Bunny Warren *just* the way she is. Half the male patients are nuts about her—and do you know why? Because she isn't brainy, or opinionated, or adorned with school certificates. She's kind and lovable and sincere and she makes a better nurse than you can ever hope to!'

Unexpectedly, the student nurse subsided into tears just as the door opened and admitted Staff Nurse Connell.

'What's all this?' she asked.

The student nurse sobbed more loudly. Nurse Taylor opened her mouth and closed it angrily. Bunny made a helpless gesture.

'It's me,' she said. 'I don't know why, but I started talking about the dance—and being glamorous—and then everything seemed to go up in smoke!'

Hope put her hand upon the student nurse's shoulder and gave her a gentle shake. 'Snap out of that,' she said quietly. 'Remember, when you feel like howling, that there are patients out in the ward who feel a great deal worse. What you want is a job of real hard work. There's nothing better for getting tears or temper out of the system! Off you go to the sluice. There's plenty waiting there.'

'I came here to be a nurse—to study and pass my exams—not to be a domestic drudge!' the girl sobbed.

'So did we all, but if we don't take the

drudgery in our stride, all the exams in the world won't help us. Off you go. And clean out the sterilizer while you're there.'

With something between a sob and a wail the girl departed. Hope controlled her desire to laugh. All along, the girl had been a bit of a headache, full of ideas which, one by one, were being pricked like burst balloons. One met this type of student occasionally—full of theories and ideals, and the more they had excelled at school, the worse they were. Coming down to earth was harder then.

'As for you, Nurse Taylor, count ten every time you feel like losing your temper. It helps.'

'I'd need to count a hundred to keep my temper with her.' Taylor muttered. 'Started advising Bunny how to glamorize herself, if you please!'

And suddenly they were laughing, all three of them, Bunny most of all. 'Glamorous—*me!*' she choked. 'Bless the child, I do believe she really meant to help me!'

'I could stand her if she weren't so darned smug,' said Taylor. *'I'd advise you to wear dark colors, in order to detract from your size,'* she mimicked.

'Is that what she said?' Hope asked.

'She did, indeed—and meant it!'

'Oh well,' said Bunny philosophically, 'it takes all sorts to make a world. What are you wearing tonight, Nurse Connell?'

'Same old blue. I thought I might be able to

afford a new one this season, but no luck. Faith's been fiddling around with it, though. I don't know what she's been up to—won't let me see it, she says, until tonight.'

'She's clever with her hands, that sister of yours. It always seems surprising to me that she should be so artistic, and yet have a scientific brain. She's blossomed lately, don't you think?'

Hope did think so—and knew why. Faith hadn't admitted it yet; in fact, she had clung almost desperately to her pose of indifference toward the chief pathologist, but she wouldn't be able to keep it much longer, Hope knew. Once or twice she had dropped into the laboratory on some pretext or other, and found Charles and her sister deep in conversation. It always seemed to be clinical or scientific, but from their eyes they might have been listening to heavenly music.

'Is it true that Charity's dog was run over in the park yesterday?' Taylor asked.

Hope's face clouded. 'Poor old Mustard—yes, it's true. A van delivering goods to the park café hit him and broke both his forelegs. He'll be all right, though. Fortunately, Doctor Shearing was around—'

'He is always around if Charity is,' Bunny commented. 'D'you know what I think? I think he's in love with her.'

Hope thought so, too. Indeed, she hoped so.

'He's not so bad as we thought at first, is

he?' Nurse Taylor commented. 'I mean, he seemed so forbidding, somehow, but really he's quite human. The patients like him.'

'So will the staff, in time,' said Hope.

'I heard he was on the carpet for telling Caroline Ransom to go home. I wonder what happened?'

'I know what *should* have happened,' Bunny remarked caustically. 'He should have been given St. Bede's Order of Merit—for courage. No one else seemed to have the nerve to do it. Certainly not Doctor Stacey.'

Nurse Taylor's eyes opened wide then.

'My dears, have you *heard* about Stacey? Made a mistaken diagnosis in Matthew ward. I'd love to have been a fly on the wall when he owned up about it!'

Bunny asked, agog: 'Will he get the sack, d'you think?'

'Oh, no!' Hope protested. 'Surely not! A mistake is a mistake, but this one can be rectified, from all I hear. I expect it taught him a lesson, though,' she added thoughtfully, 'and one he won't forget.'

'What I can't imagine,' said Nurse Taylor, 'is how he ever plucked up courage to face the super. He couldn't say boo to a goose!'

She broke off abruptly, staring at the door. It had swung upon its soundless hinges to admit Doctor Stacey himself. Dull color flooded his face, then subsided. He said frigidly, but with a firmness they had never heard before: 'I'm looking for Sister. She isn't in the ward. I want to know if she has had that blood test on the leukemia patient in number five. Tell her to let me know, will you?'

He departed, then, quite coolly. Taylor let out a soundless whistle. 'What's happened to him?' she whispered hoarsely. 'It's always: "Would you mind asking Sister" or "If Sister would be so kind"!'

'Whatever has happened,' commented Bunny, 'it's an improvement.'

Hope said: 'I must get along. Taylor, help me with the surgical trolley, will you? I want to get away on time tonight. Charity hasn't got Mustard to guide her across the courtyard, and although she insists that she can manage, I'd like to be going off duty at the same time.'

'I'll prepare it now, Nurse,' Taylor answered, and Hope left the kitchen and went toward Caroline Ransom's ward. That young lady was due to leave this afternoon. Her mother's car was collecting her. When Hope entered, the girl was dressed and looking extremely pretty—and extremely bored and resentful. Nothing had worked out as she planned. Not a doctor here had fallen in love with her or even shown the slightest willingness to flirt with her. It had been a very dull visit, after all. As for that business over young Doctor Shearing, it seemed to have fizzled out like flat champagne. He was walking about the hospital as large as life—she had even heard him laughing in the corridor this morning.

Worse than that—he had put his head round the door to say goodbye, and his expression was more than cheerful. It was alive and vigorous and extremely happy; happier than she had ever seen it.

'So you're off,' he said. 'You'll be glad, once you are home. And thank you for vacating the bed—it is needed for an urgent case.'

There was absolutely nothing she could take offense at in that remark. It was courteous, unresentful—and final. And he didn't seem the least upset when she turned her back coldly. He went on his way, whistling.

All things considered, Caroline felt extremely sorry for herself. Bother Felicity! she thought. She *would* come along with some exaggerated story about Michael Shearing and his mother and leave me to make a fool of myself! But I'll get even with her, somehow . . .

'All ready to go?' Hope asked pleasantly. Caroline muttered that she was and that she wished to goodness the car would arrive.

As if in answer to her wish, the door opened and there, surprisingly, stood Felicity. 'My word!' sneered Caroline. 'You're playing the affectionate sister a bit too much, aren't you?' She turned to Staff Nurse Connell and said viciously: 'Tell me, does the nursing staff really believe Mrs. Drake comes here out of concern for me? Because if so, let me disillusion you!

She comes merely in the hope of meeting Phillip Trent around the place. Occasionally you have, haven't you, Felicity dear? Perhaps Nurse Connell will be able to tell you if he's about this afternoon.'

Felicity's eyes narrowed into betraying slits of anger.

'If you're ready,' she said furiously, 'the car is outside.'

She turned upon her heel and walked away. Her young sister could not have humiliated her more—especially in front of that red-haired nurse. Caroline had made it seem as if she—*she*, Felicity Drake, for whom men fell like ninepins—was running after the surgeon! As if she had ever done such a thing!

By the time she reached the main hall, Felicity's anger had calmed a little. One thing was certain—Nurse Connell had seen quite plainly, the other evening, just how the land lay, just how important she was in Phillip's life, so that if she cherished any secret ambitions about marrying him, she must know how futile they were.

Phillip is mine, *mine!* she thought angrily. He has always belonged to me. He will never belong to anyone else!

* * *

Faith had worked miracles with Hope's 'old blue.' She'd slashed away the shoulders and, to soften the plunging neckline, slanted a mist of petunias, in shades varying from gentian to palest blue, across the bodice. Layers of gossamer tulle concealed the foundation, like a summer cloud.

She'd been busy on Charity's behalf, too, transforming last winter's white organza. A yellow velvet sash; a cluster of mimosa for her hair; the hem of the billowing skirt caught up to reveal a bright, rustling flash of daffodil yellow—and Charity looked like a breath of spring. She touched the skirt with her sensitive hands; felt the sash, the flowers, the taffeta underslip, and said with a radiant smile: 'I feel wonderful!'

'You look wonderful, darling,' Faith told her.

And so she did. There was more than spring in Charity's radiance this evening. There was the promise of summer and sweet fulfilment—like a rose about to bloom.

Something had happened to Charity. Something was still happening. And, thought Hope shrewdly, it was going to continue happening all through her life. Happiness held out its arms toward her, guiding her faltering steps, leading her to glory. Happiness—or young Doctor Shearing. Or both.

'What about you, Faith?' Hope asked. 'You've been so busy with Charity and me, you can't have had time to do a thing for yourself.'

'Oh, but I have!' Faith's lovely smile peeped

out. 'I've been wildly extravagant and reckless. I've bought myself a new one!'

The excited exclamations of her sisters drove her to her wardrobe where, amidst a breathless hush, she drew forth a hanger, draped in a dust cover. Whisking the sheet aside, she held her prize aloft.

'Ooh!' sighed Hope. 'It's heavenly! Just *heavenly!*'

Charity's hand reached forth and touched the new gown. It felt exquisite. 'What sort of material is it?' she asked, for the texture was unfamiliar.

'Lamé. Silver. All glistening and wonderful,' Hope answered. 'Faith, you've never worn anything like this!'

'I know.'

She didn't add that that was why she had bought it—because she felt like a new sort of person lately, and wanted something in keeping with her new personality. Nor did she add the other reason for her purchase—the fact that Charles had come into the laboratory yesterday and said: 'I've seen the perfect gown for you, Faith. You know that exclusive shop in the Square—'

'Fenella, you mean? I've window-shopped there, many times.'

'Go and window-shop again. It's all by itself, in regal splendor, on a sort of dais in the middle. And it's *you,* Faith.'

And it was, Why she had known it, the

moment she saw the gown, she could not tell. She had always worn simple, rather unsophisticated clothes, but this had a brilliance and splendor about it which seemed to reflect the shining wonder which, day by day, was increasing within her. When, greatly daring, she tried it on, the salesgirl had gasped in admiration.

It fitted like a glove—smooth, sleek, slender, revealing the beauty of a figure which spent most of its life concealed by a white tailored coverall. The rich darkness of her hair was emphasized by its brilliance. She needed no jewels—which was fortunate, she thought wryly, since she possessed none. She knew instinctively that, no matter what it cost, she had to have this gown. It seemed an omen, a symbol of a future which was suddenly brilliant with promise.

By seven o'clock the nurses' home buzzed with excitement. Over in the wards the night nurses grumbled. 'It wouldn't be a bad idea,' said one, 'to fit silencers on the patients' bells; then we could *all* go to the dance and forget about them!' But someone had to be on night duty. The pulse of the hospital still beat. Perhaps, next year, if one were lucky . . .

Up in the residents' room, a man sat alone. Dancing wasn't in his line and, besides, he didn't feel like going. It was the first time for years that he had failed to put in an appearance, dancing duty dances with the staff, with committee wives, with all the people who mattered; being polite and agreeable and charming. Now he didn't care. It just wasn't worth the effort.

Of course his absence would be noticed—and commented upon. 'Stacey isn't here!' they'd say, and finish with a significant whisper: 'Of course, you know why, don't you?'

But they'd all be wrong, all the giggling nurses and gossiping sisters and the medicals as well. And later, when additional speculation broke out, they'd be wrong again. And he just wouldn't care.

He felt an extraordinary sense of relief; newly invigorated and free. It was illogical and entirely unreasonable, but it was there. He had plunged into the deep end and surfaced, to his own surprise. It gave him courage to do it again. He hadn't drowned, after all.

The door opened and a young man entered. It was Michael Shearing, and he looked extremely handsome in his immaculate tails. There was something else that was arresting about him, too—an air of self-confidence through happiness, instead of aggression. When he smiled it was completely natural and without bitterness—an open, honest smile.

'Ah, Shearing—out to enjoy yourself tonight?'

'I hope, very much.'

'Taking anyone?' asked Stacey, to whom the little affairs between doctors and nurses had never really appealed. But now, to his own surprise, he really was interested.

'Charity Connell. The physiotherapist.'

'The blind girl! Can she dance?'

'I don't know. I intend to teach her, if not.' There was so much he wanted to do for her. He wanted to take care of her always, to lead her through life safely and happily, to love her.

'I expect she can,' Doctor Stacey observed. 'She's amazingly self-reliant, so much so that one forgets she cannot see.'

Michael smiled gently, proudly.

'Aren't you coming to the dance, Doctor?'

'Not I. I've traipsed round that town hall floor year after year, not really enjoying it. I've finished with all that. In fact, Shearing, I may as well tell you now that I hope, before long, to finish with St. Bede's.'

Michael stared.

'You don't mean—'

'No—I don't mean that I've been fired, although I daresay the whole hospital will believe that when I go. The super. was surprisingly decent this morning.'

'He seems a very reasonable sort of man,' Michael said tactfully.

'He is. As supers go, I'd say he's above average.'

Stacey paused, remembering his chief's reaction and remembering, too, the extraordinary expression upon his face, even as he passed inevitable judgment upon him—an expression of pleased surprise because his subordinate had the courage to come along and admit his mistake. He didn't think, before, that I had much courage, Stacey thought with renewed perception. All the same, I'm glad he didn't spare me his opinion of my error. I needed a lashing like that, to wake me up . . .

Aloud, he said: 'I've decided to look for a new appointment, Shearing. A man can stay at one hospital too long. I should have dug my roots up long ago. I need transplanting; fresh soil.'

'I'm sure—' Michael began uncertainly, but Stacey cut him short.

'Oh, I'll have a good reference from the super! I'm "conscientious." He won't be able to say more than that. My qualifications are good and I'll find a new appointment all right. But I want something more adventurous, believe it or not. I've applied for a Mission hospital, in Uganda. They're crying out for doctors, and the life isn't easy. It's what I want, what I need. As for you,' he smiled suddenly, 'you'll get my job with ease—'

'That's ridiculous! I haven't been here five minutes and I've already been on the mat.'

'And acquitted yourself well, apparently. Off you go to your dance, and enjoy yourself. This time next year you'll be visiting it in the capacity of senior physician—you see if I'm not right.'

He waved a friendly hand as Michael

departed.

* * *

Somehow—Agatha was never quite sure just how—Felicity was included in their party. Felicity got herself included in any party of which Phillip was a member. They arrived at the town hall just as Matron and John Benham drove up in the secretary's small car. They were a nice-looking couple—middle-aged and kindly, and devoted to one another with the affection of a lifetime. Why Agatha should notice that at this precise moment she really did not know, but the way in which John Benham handed Matron out of his car was somehow significant.

Phillip turned and slipped his hand beneath Agatha's elbow, a gesture which comforted and reassured her. In comparison with Felicity she felt unsophisticated and inferior. Did Phillip realize that? Was that why he paid especial attention to his sister this evening? For that was precisely what he did, as if he wanted to atone, somehow, for bringing Felicity along.

His first dance was with Agatha, a fact which filled her with a quite ridiculous happiness—especially when she glimpsed Felicity's expression as they moved onto the floor. She was angry. But then, it didn't take much to make Felicity angry. Thwart her in the slightest degree, and she became a vixen. Phillip was an observant man—couldn't he see that? Couldn't he sense it?

She was right in one thing at least—Phillip's acute observation. The first thing he had seen, when they entered the ballroom, was the copper head of Hope Connell against the black shoulder of the resident surgical officer. They were dancing together—and dancing rather intimately, thought Phillip jealously. The R.S.O.'s cheek was very close to hers, his head stooping toward her lovely face, his arm unnecessarily tight about her waist.

It was a very tiny waist, Phillip observed—smaller than it looked in uniform. Her shoulders were white and beautiful above the strapless gown, rising from a mist of heavenly blue. Was it her clear, pale skin which enabled her to wear that particular shade?

When the dance ended they were very near to the couple. Phillip saw the man's glance as he released Hope, and a wave of anger ran through him. Fatuous, that was what it was. Fatuous and self-satisfied and decidedly amorous. Phillip did not like it at all.

Taking his sister back to their own table, he saw Felicity talking to the medical superintendent, who was also with their party. Matron and John Benham joined them. There would be polite conversation, and a round of duty dances throughout the evening. And the whole thing, thought Phillip suddenly, would be flat and boring and exasperating.

But the exasperation would come from the fact that, only a few tables away, Hope Connell sat next to the R.S.O., his arm along the back of her chair. There was quite a party of them, he observed—her two sisters, both looking particularly lovely, Charles Willstack and, a moment later, Michael Shearing. He came a little late, walked straight across to Charity and asked her to dance.

Felicity was saying in a tone of surprise: 'Really, some of these little nurses get themselves up quite well, considering . . .'

'Considering what?' Phillip asked abruptly.

'Considering women who wear uniform all day have so little taste when out of it.'

'That isn't true at all!' he exclaimed angrily. 'Look at the Connell sisters—look at the little blind girl, like a breath of spring, and the dark one, exquisite in silver . . .'

'And the redhead?' Felicity purred.

'She isn't a redhead,' he answered softly. 'That hair is the color of autumn leaves—absolutely glorious.'

'Really, darling, for a medical man you're becoming quite poetical . . . Shall we dance?'

'Forgive me, Felicity—Matron next.' It was all in the line of duty, by order of precedence, but Felicity resented it. She was clutching at anger to stifle the unfamiliar sense of fear which was beating like a hammer in her heart. She watched Phillip move onto the floor, steering Matron in a gentle cloud of grey chiffon—like an elephant draped in a cobweb, Felicity thought maliciously—but his eyes wandered above his partner's head, scanning the ballroom, searching among the dancers, and, instinctively, Felicity knew for whom he searched.

Now she was definitely frightened. She had the awful feeling that something was going to go wrong. Should she invent some excuse—a headache, perhaps—and persuade Phillip to take her home? Anything to get him away from here, away from that nurse with hair the color of autumn leaves . . .

When, at last, they danced together, Felicity let her figure lean gently and invitingly against him. In the old days, when he had been so madly in love with her before her marriage to Marcus, Phillip would have been stirred—and she would have known it. Now she knew with a sickening sense of shock that he was not stirred at all.

She whispered: 'Darling—' but he didn't seem to hear. He had become so familiar with the endearment that it passed him by. She repeated it, urgently, and he jerked his mind from wherever it had been wandering and looked down at her.

'You haven't admired my dress, Phillip.'

'Haven't I? It's lovely, of course, but anything you wear is lovely, Felicity. You have excellent taste.'

She said mockingly: 'Thank you, Phillip. Is that all you have to say?'

'Should there be anything else?'

'That you love me—perhaps.'

He made no answer, and fear beat with urgent wings against her heart.

'Phillip!' Her voice was sharp. 'Don't you think it's about time we discussed the future, you and I?'

He evaded: 'This is hardly the time or the place, surely?'

'Then let's go home to my flat.'

'You know I can't. This is an official appearance, Felicity.'

'Then afterwards—'

'Afterwards I'm going straight home to bed, my girl. I'm due in the theatre tomorrow morning. Fatigue is a surgeon's worst enemy.'

She pouted prettily, but he did not even see it, because he was watching a couple disappearing through tall windows on to a balcony outside. How like Barlow, he thought angrily, to take a girl out of a hot ballroom into an autumn night! He wanted to drop his partner abruptly and hurry after them, to tell that confounded surgical officer just what he thought of him, to ask Hope why she let him take her outside . . .

Hope was wondering that herself. She didn't really want to admire the view of the coast which, Stephen insisted, she really should see from the town hall. Once outside, of course, he put his arms round her. 'You might catch cold,' he said softly, and she felt his face coming down to hers. She wanted to push him away, but did not. What did it matter? Phillip was here, and he hadn't even greeted her. He hadn't even seen her. He had brought Felicity with him, and Felicity looked so wonderful that by comparison she felt gauche and drab, even in the gown Faith's clever fingers had transformed.

A flash of silver passed the windows—Faith dancing by with Charles, of course. Briefly, Hope saw her sister's face upturned to his. He was smiling at her gently and saying something . . .

* * *

'You bought it, Faith—the dress I liked so much. The dress I said was "you." '

She laughed shakily. 'And mortgaged a month's salary to do so!'

'Why?' he whispered.

'Because I liked it, too,' she answered lightly.

'No other reason?'

'Could there be?'

'You could have bought it *because* I liked it. It is the kind of dress I will choose for you when I come with you to buy your clothes.'

She trembled, and he continued quietly:

'Because I shall, you know, when we are

married. I'm the sort of man who likes to buy his wife's clothes.'

'You sound as if you've had plenty of practice!'

She was still trembling. He could hear it in her voice and feel it within the crook of his arm.

'Not yet,' he told her, 'but I intend to. With you. I've waited a long time, and only for you, Faith . . . and I give you fair warning that unless you surrender soon, unless you stop resisting me, I'll take the law into my own hands and carry you off . . .'

She chuckled. The chuckle grew into laughter—happy, delighted laughter. He had known, from the beginning, that one day he would make her laugh like this. 'What's the joke?' He grinned. 'Don't you know a woman should always share her jokes with the man she marries?'

'Just the picture of you, with a condensing flask in one hand and me in the other, dashing for the border in your white coverall, and dashing back again to the laboratory the moment the ring is on my finger . . .'

He laughed and held her closer. 'I'm dashed if I intend to spend my honeymoon amongst guinea-pigs! Or *your* honeymoon, either. I'll share it with no one but you—understand?'

Someone bumped into them—the back of a man's broad shoulders. It was Michael. 'Sorry!' he laughed, and held Charity more closely.

As they danced on Michael said: 'Men in love shouldn't go on a dance floor. There's Charles absorbed in Faith, and myself absorbed in you—it isn't fair to the rest of the dancers. Shall we leave the floor to them? Shall we find somewhere nice and private? I've something to tell you . . .'

He led her out to his car. They drove along the coast road. When they stopped finally, he said: 'You know I love you, don't you, Charity?'

He heard her little fluttering breath, and was surprised by her answer.

'Why?' she said.

'*Why?* Because you *are* you—no other reason, except that you're all the things I've ever wanted and ever shall want; all the things I didn't believe existed. Sweetness and sincerity and beauty, all rolled into one.'

'Beauty?' she echoed. 'I've never wondered whether I had beauty or not . . .'

'Perhaps that is why you have so much.' He took her in his arms and kissed her with gentle reverence. 'I love you so much that it will take my whole life-time to tell you about it. So, you see, you will have to marry me to give me the opportunity . . .'

He felt her withdrawal, and was immediately alarmed.

'What is it, my darling? What is the matter?'

'You're forgetting something, Michael. I am blind. And a blind wife would be a handicap . . .'

'You could never be a handicap to anyone,' he told her. 'The reverse, in fact. I want to marry you because I love you—just as you are. I wouldn't have you any different. To me, your eyes are the loveliest in the world, because they see only the goodness in life, and in people. Because they are true and steady and sincere.'

'You don't pity me, Michael?' Her sensitive hands reached up and silenced his swift answer. 'Think carefully—it was because I was afraid of pity that I asked why you wanted to marry me. Pity isn't love, you know . . .'

'All compassionate and tender feelings are part of love—but no, I don't pity you, Charity. How can I? You have given me strength and understanding and more besides—you have given me back my heart.'

Later, he said reluctantly: 'I suppose we must go—'

'Yes, Michael.'

'But not back to the dance. Not yet. There is somewhere I want to take you first.'

'Where?' she asked with interest.

'To meet my parents. You know one already, and she loves you. The other will love you, too. I think it will be safe to interrupt them, now . . .'

'Michael!'

He nodded, and smiled.

'Yes—I took my mother home tonight. She

was afraid, I think, but not when she saw my father's face. I think perhaps he was afraid, too, although he remembered he was once a soldier and tried to hide the fact. But he couldn't hide anything when he saw her—neither his fear, nor his love, nor his unutterable relief.' He mused gently: 'It was funny, Charity, how that museum of a house became a home again, the moment she entered . . .'

Agatha said: 'Where's Phillip?'

Felicity scowled.

'I can't imagine. After our dance he dumped me back here at the table and stalked off toward the balcony. I suppose he wanted a breath of air. I can't say I blame him. It is stifling in here.'

But it wasn't air Phillip sought. He opened the balcony window and walked determinedly through it.

'Barlow!' he commanded angrily.

The man jerked away from his partner—who, Phillip observed, let him go quite willingly. Had she even been trying to reject him? It was difficult to tell, in the dim light.

Stephen Barlow, flushed and embarrassed, said: 'Yes, sir?'

'What about doing a few duty dances? The medical staff are, I believe, expected to make themselves affable at these affairs—but not to the point of exposing the nurses to the chill night air!'

Hope stifled a laugh. He heard it quite distinctly. Barlow answered with a touch of bravado: 'I was endeavoring to avoid that, sir!' but he departed, nevertheless, casting a dark glance at the honorary surgeon's broad back.

When he had gone, Phillip said furiously: 'He was kissing you!'

'He was trying to, I admit, sir,' Hope answered demurely.

'And you didn't repulse him?'

'Should I?' she asked innocently. 'Isn't it rather unkind to repulse a man in love?'

'So he *is* in love with you?'

'So he declares, sir.'

'Stop addressing me in that ridiculous way! We are not in the wards now. You know perfectly well that my name is Phillip.'

'Yes, Phillip,' she answered meekly, and shivered.

'You are cold!'

'As you yourself observed, sir, the night air is a little chill . . .'

He moved toward her.

'Perhaps I should go back to the ballroom!' she said swiftly.

'Why? I am as capable as any other man of protecting a woman from the cold.'

To prove his claim, he demonstrated his ability. From the depths of his shoulder she managed to gulp: 'Felicity!'

'What about Felicity?'

'She'll be wondering where you are.

Shouldn't you be dancing with her?'

'I've done all my dances for the evening. The rest I intend to be for pleasure—my own pleasure. And yours, I hope.'

'Mine, sir?'

'Since they are all to be shared with you, I sincerely hope so.'

He felt her slim body shake with laughter. Her voice mocked him.

'I had no idea you were so masterful, sir.'

'Phillip!'

'Phillip, then,' she echoed softly, and laughed no more.

A shadow fell across the window. A woman stood there. Hope recognized Felicity's lovely figure and tried to jerk away, but Phillip's hold was too strong.

'Really!' Felicity said harshly. 'I've always heard that doctors flirted with nurses, but don't you think this is being a little indiscreet, Phillip?'

'I can see nothing indiscreet,' said Phillip, 'about proposing to the girl I hope to marry. I prefer to do it in private, rather than in public, but I am perfectly willing to continue the discussion, if Hope so prefers it, in the ballroom . . .'

'Anywhere, Phillip! Anywhere at all!' Hope's voice was radiantly happy. 'I can say "yes' while we are dancing or shout it from the housetops, if you wish.'

'That,' said Phillip, 'sounds like a wonderful

idea . . .'

Felicity turned upon her heel and walked furiously back to their table.

'I have a headache!' she declared. 'Will someone please take me home?'

Agatha regarded her with maternal concern. 'My dear, I'm so sorry—it must be the heat.'

'Yes. The heat!' Felicity snapped.

Agatha's eyes went past her to the dance floor, and her heart leaped. It wasn't the heat which had provoked Felicity's headache. It was the expression upon Phillip's face as he looked down into Hope's. What a wonderful world it was! Agatha thought happily. What a really *wonderful* world!